NILS
DISCOVERS
AMERICA

Adventures with Erik

By Julie Jensen McDonald

Penfield
Press

About the Author

Julie Jensen McDonald has published eight novels, a biography, a regional history, four collections of ethnic material, and two inspirational books. She is a graduate of the University of Iowa and attended the Iowa Writers' Workshop. A member of the faculty of St. Ambrose University, Davenport, Iowa, she also teaches in the Summer Writing Festival at the University of Iowa. Her own Scandinavian heritage and her deep admiration for Norway and the Norwegians prompted the creation of Nils the Nisse. Julie and her husband Elliott have four granddaughters and a Scottish deerhound puppy.

About the Illustrator

Norma Wangsness, a Norwegian-American artist, used the details of historic artifacts of the Viking age to enhance her drawings of the Norse gods. Her artistic skills include painting and rosemaling. She and her husband Willis live in Decorah, Iowa, where Norma serves as a volunteer for Vesterheim, the Norwegian-American museum.

Books by Mail

Nils Discovers America: Adventures with Erik
(This book) Postpaid: $9.95; 2 for $16; 3 for $24.
Please send for a complete list of books.
(Prices subject to change).

Penfield Press
215 Brown Street
Iowa City, Iowa 52245

© 1990 Julie Jensen McDonald
ISBN 0-941016-74-9
Library of Congress Number 90-60678

Contents

The Long Road Led Here

*Erik Dahl and Nils the Nisse across the street
from Vesterheim,
the Norwegian-American Museum at
Decorah, Iowa*

Nils Comes to Vesterheim

The Norwegian-American Museum

Nils the Nisse
A Nisse is a Norwegian elf

Once upon a time (not so very long ago) a nisse named Nils woke up from a long, long sleep and asked, "Where am I?"

A human face was looking at him, but the sounds coming from the mouth seemed strange.

Nils shut his eyes quickly and snuggled back into the woven stuff in the old chest. Perhaps this human would think he was a doll and leave him alone.

"Hey, Ed," the human said. "Look what I found."

Nils opened his eyes just a slit and saw another human face looming above the chest. It smiled.

"Wow! Look at the detail on that figure! Let's show it during the school visit. The kids will love it."

"We can't do that," the other human said. "This stuff isn't even catalogued. I'll bet that chest hasn't been opened for a hundred years."

5

Human time meant nothing to Nils. Nisser keep their own time. And they have special powers. He could understand these humans, even if they weren't speaking Norwegian.

He was shaking off more than a century of sleep, and everything came back to him now.

Most nisser were perfectly happy in their nice homes under barns and unoccupied buildings in Norway. Not Nils. He wanted to live among people, but when he approached humans, they were terrified. From the way they reacted to him, you would have thought he were a troll—one of the bad guys in the old stories. Some trolls were ugly with three heads and just one eye, the stories said. They were big and stupid and did dumb things like throwing boulders at church bells to stop their ringing.

Nils wanted the world to know that some nisser were happy, good-natured and helpful. They were much smaller than humans, actually.

And instead of one eye to be popped in and out of three heads the way the trolls did it, each nisse had two perfectly normal eyes. A few three-headed trolls had disrupted some nisser family reunions, so Nils knew how awful they were.

Some of the nisser were troublemakers, always playing tricks on people. They weren't as nasty as the trolls, but bad enough, and that made things hard for the well-intentioned nisser.

Nils really tried to make friends with Norwegian humans. He stepped out on a mountain road with a friendly wave, but the humans, expecting some nasty prank, screamed and whipped their horses to a gallop.

Finally, he went to the town of Kristiansund and peeked in all the windows, looking for a family that would accept him. The humans he liked best were the Dahls, a family packing to go to America. Nils liked the ring of their laughter and the kindness in their eyes. He decided to go to America with them. When the women weren't looking, he jumped into the big chest decorated with rosemaling and covered himself with the shawls inside.

Even a nisse can get seasick, so when the ship began to pitch and toss on the ocean, Nils put himself to sleep with a magic spell.

A sharp, ringing sound startled Nils now. He heard the human say, "Vesterheim Norwegian-American Museum." Nils's nisse sense told him what the human was hearing through the telephone receiver pressed to his ear.

"Are you ready for two busloads of fifth graders?"

"Almost. I just opened a chest somebody brought in and found a wonderful nisse figure. I wish we could get it ready for display before you come."

"Couldn't we just take a look? The director is out of town, isn't he?"

"Yeah, but I don't like to break the rules."

"Suit yourself. See you at 1:30."

Nils leaped out of the chest. He wanted to escape before the human came back and closed the lid. He had forgotten how wonderful it was to breathe fresh air. He ran around the corner on his short, little legs and hid behind a round chair carved from a log.

The humans stayed in the other room, and he finally decided to be comfortable. He climbed up and sat in the round log chair as he had done so often in Norway.

The humans went off to lunch, and now Nils could look around the museum. He went into the Selland-Forde log house and set the wooden cradle rocking. He looked at the mittens and gloves with their bright embroidery. He tilted the copper tea kettle in the corner fireplace.

Then he went back to the round wooden chair and put his nisse powers to work to find out what had happened to the Dahls, the family that brought him across the sea.

He saw it all—how they came to this place where Norwegians had settled. He saw how hard they worked and how happily they danced to the music of the Hardanger fiddle. He saw how Mette Dahl, the mother of the family, sighed over the loss of the trunk decorated with rosemaling. Her husband, Halvor, said he would make her a new one, and he did.

Nils sits in the wooden chair, a kubbestal,
at the Vesterheim Museum

Meanwhile, the trunk where Nils slept sat in a railroad baggage room for many years. When trains no longer came to the station, bats and birds came in through broken windows and perched on the chest, but no one ever opened the lid to awaken Nils.

Finally, the station was to be torn down. One of the workmen saw the dusty, cobweb-covered chest and put it in his truck. He sold it to an antique dealer. She started to open it, but when a large spider scuttled out, she quickly closed the lid and decided to give the chest and all its contents to the Vesterheim Museum. She could use the tax deduction. Her assistant put the chest into her station wagon, and she drove immediately to Decorah in northeast Iowa.

Nils's nisse sense told him that many generations of Dahls had lived in these parts, and they continued to be the kind, happy people who had impressed him in Kristiansund so long ago.

Nils looked out into the street and saw automobiles for the first time. He wondered what they ate, and then his nisse sense told him that they drank gasoline.

Two huge, yellow buses were stopping outside. Noisy children poured out of them and ran toward the museum. Nils jumped down from his chair and hid behind it.

The museum humans were back from lunch to greet the school group. The teacher was telling the children not to touch anything.

One boy caught Nils's attention. He was backing away from a bigger boy, who was stepping on his foot and pinching him. The smaller boy made no sound as he tried to escape. The bully came after him, stomping and pinching.

"Stop it, or I'll tell the teacher," the smaller boy whispered.

"Just try it! I'll get you after school!"

The smaller boy hung back as the group moved to another part of the museum.

"Pssst!" said Nils, emerging from behind the chair.

The boy stared at him in amazement.

"What's your name?" Nils asked. He could have used his nisse sense to find out, but he knew how to be polite.

"Erik. What's yours?"

"Nils. I'm a nisse."

"What's that?" Erik asked.

"The closest word in your language is 'elf,' and that's not quite it. Anyhow, I'm not your average nisse."

"Whatever," said Erik. "You're the first one *I* ever met."

"Look, can we be friends?" Nils asked. "I never could get very close to humans in Norway, but maybe it's different here."

Erik held out his hand and they shook on it. "I don't have very many friends. I'm the runt of the class, and they pick on me."

"So I noticed," said Nils. "But we'll fix that. I want you to do exactly what I say."

"OK," said Erik.

"Go into the next room with the rest of the class and stand

9

next to the boy who pinched you."

"I'm already black and blue!" Erik protested.

"Just do it."

The teacher was coming back to see what had happened to Erik, and Nils had to turn on his nisse magic in a hurry to keep her from seeing him. He became invisible.

"Come along, Erik," the teacher said. "Stay with the rest of the class."

Erik joined the others and went over to the boy who had picked on him.

"How are you doing, Bobby?" he said.

"I'll show you!" Bobby said, bringing his pinching fingers close to Erik's arm.

Suddenly his fingers were squeezed together. He couldn't open them. Nils held them in a nisse grip.

"Hey!" Bobby yelled in terror.

"Stomp on his foot, Erik," Nils said, and Erik did.

"Ow!" yelled Bobby.

"What is going on here?" the teacher asked.

"I can't open my hand!" Bobby sniffled. "And Erik stepped on my foot."

One of the girls said, "Bobby stomped on Erik's foot first."

Nils whispered in Erik's ear, "Tell him you'll open his fingers if he promises never to bother you again."

"Bobby," Erik said. "Promise you'll never bother me again, and I'll turn your hand loose."

"You've got nothing to do with my hand!" Bobby scoffed.

"Then just stay that way for the rest of your life," Erik said, feeling bolder than he ever had been.

Bobby started to cry, and the teacher tried to pry his fingers apart.

"Bobby," she said crossly. "Stop this nonsense and open your fingers!"

"I can't!" he shrieked.

Some of the other boys tried to pry his fingers apart, but they couldn't do it either.

"All you have to do is promise," Erik said, crossing his arms and waiting.

Bobby screwed up his face, and the words came out between clenched teeth. "All right, I promise."

Nils released the fingers, and Bobby flexed his hand in amazement.

"How did you do that, Erik?" asked Jenny, who was the smartest girl in the class, and also the prettiest and the most fun.

"I had a little help from a friend," said Erik, looking around and wondering where the invisible Nils might be. Then his own hand started to move as the nisse clasped it in friendship.

He heard the nisse voice whisper, "Take me home with you," and he nodded happily.

From that day on, things would be different, Erik decided. Nils had let him take the credit for super-gluing Bobby's fingers and getting them apart again. Nobody would mess with a kid who could do that!

And if anybody called him a runt now, he really wouldn't mind. After all, his friend Nils was much smaller.

Nils Meets the Dahls

As the school group was leaving Vesterheim Museum, Nils saw the humans who had opened the trunk talking together. They looked worried.

"I can't find that nisse figure anywhere, Ed. Did you put it somewhere?"

"I didn't touch it," the other human said. "It couldn't walk off by itself. Maybe we'd better check the kids."

Time for a bit of nisse magic, thought Nils, who was still invisible. He squeezed his eyes shut and concentrated, erasing the memory of a nisse in a chest from the minds of both humans.

"What were we talking about, Ed?" the first human asked, looking puzzled.

Ed scratched his head. "Did I ask you if you wanted to go to the basketball game in Iowa City Saturday? I've got an extra ticket."

"Hey, all right!"

Nils grinned and hurried after Erik.

"Are you there, Nils?" Erik whispered.

"Right beside you," Nils said, leaping up to tug at the hood on Erik's jacket.

They climbed onto the bus, and Nils had to hurry up the steps to keep from being trampled by the other kids. Erik slid into a seat, and Nils hopped up beside him.

"I'll put my jacket here to keep anyone from sitting on you," Erik said.

Just then, Jenny, the girl Erik liked best, sat down and began to slide over. She'd never paid much attention to Erik before, and now, he wished she wouldn't. She was going to squash Nils!

"Move your coat," she said.

Erik picked up the coat, but he put his arm out to protect his new friend.

"What's the matter with you, Erik?" she asked. "We're supposed to sit three to a seat!"

"We are!" he said, looking miserable.

"Mrs. Anderson," Jenny called to the teacher, "Erik won't move over!"

"I'll be there in a minute, Jenny," said the teacher, who was busy settling some mischief in the back seat.

Nils whispered, "I'll sit on the back of the seat near the window and dangle my feet over your shoulder. Don't worry, I won't kick!"

Erik moved his arm, giving Jenny and her friend Amy plenty of room. He could feel Nils's firm, little heels against his shoulder.

"Now," said Mrs. Anderson. "What's the problem here?"

"Everything's OK now," said Jenny.

"Yeah," said Erik, grinning. He admired Jenny's hair, which was the color of butter and braided with all kinds of bright ribbons and rosettes. She looked like the doll in the museum, but she was a lot livelier.

"I guess you really took care of old Bobby," she said.

"I didn't really do anything," Erik said modestly.

"How did you do that? Make his fingers let go?"

Erik shrugged.

"Oh, come on! Tell me!"

"Nils?" Erik whispered desperately.

Nils hopped down from his perch and pinched Jenny's fingers together.

"Hey!" Jenny yelped.

Nils hoped that Erik would catch on, and he did.

"I can't tell you how I do it, I'll just have to show you. Turn loose!"

Jenny's fingers flew apart, and her blue eyes were round as marbles. She didn't say another word until the bus pulled into the school parking lot. Then she asked Erik if he'd like to come to her birthday party.

13

"Sure," he said happily.

As they were leaving the bus, Nils leaped up and pulled Jenny's braid, just to let her know that Erik really liked her. Erik was too shy to do it himself.

The school day was almost over, but Erik told Nils that he couldn't leave when the others did. He had detention.

"What's that?" Nils asked.

"You have to stay after school because of something you did—or didn't do. I skipped gym."

"Why?"

"Because they never let me shoot baskets. They say, 'Get a ladder, you runt!', and I'm sick of it!"

"When are you supposed to do this again?"

Erik let out a big sigh and said, "Tomorrow."

"I might like that game," Nils said.

A loud bell rang. All the kids slammed their books into their desks and rushed out the door. Erik sat quietly at his desk and waited.

"Well, Erik," Mrs. Anderson said, "I guess I'll have you clean the chalkboards."

She pointed at the big, green squares filled with words. Nils decided they must be large versions of the slates children used before his long nap.

Erik picked up a long felt eraser and began to wipe words away. When the teacher's back was turned, Nils picked up another eraser and helped.

"My, but you're speedy!" she said when she saw the blank chalkboards. "Now get a damp cloth and take that chalk dust off."

"That's the worst part," Erik whispered.

"Were you speaking to me?" Mrs. Anderson said.

"No, Ma'am." Erik went to the closet and found the cloth. He went into the hall and soaked it in the drinking fountain. Nils jumped up and wrung it out, doing a much better job than Erik usually did.

Mrs. Anderson was busy grading papers at her desk, so

she didn't see the cloth moving all by itself across the board, going so fast that it blurred.

"I'm all finished, Mrs. Anderson," Erik said. "May I go?"

She shook her head in amazement. "How did you do that so fast?"

Erik shrugged.

"Well, Erik, I'll let you go if you promise to be in gym class tomorrow."

"Oh, we will!" he said.

"We?"

"I mean—*I* will." Erik rushed out with Nils at his heels.

They cut across back yards and down alleys, and Erik explained, "It's farther this way, but I change my route every day. If I don't, Bobby and those guys jump out and beat me up."

"You don't have to worry about that anymore," Nils reminded him.

"Oh, yeah!" Erik said, feeling taller and even swaggering a bit. "I forgot."

Erik's house didn't look much like Norwegian homes, Nils thought. It was long and low with a flat roof and lots of big glass windows. He followed Erik inside.

"Mom, I'm home!" Erik called.

Sonja Dahl came out of the kitchen with a big, round cookie for her son. She held the plastic package it came from in her other hand.

"You're late," she said.

"Well, we went to the museum."

"Do you have homework?"

"Nope."

"OK. Just stick around, and as soon as Dad comes home, I'll put dinner in the microwave."

Nils couldn't pick up any cooking smells, and he didn't think Mrs. Dahl was dressed for working in the kitchen. She wore a suit and shoes with high heels.

"I'll be in my room," Erik said.

Nils was amazed at the stuff all over the floor and all over the bunk beds in Erik's room. As a young nisse, he had been somewhat messy, but never anything like this!

Erik shut the door and said, "You can stop being invisible now."

Nils snapped his fingers and came into view, stroking his white, curly beard and smoothing his silver-buttoned red jacket.

"Take off your hat and stay awhile," Erik said.

"Oh, we never take off our hats," Nils said.

"Why not?"

"Since the beginning of time, the world has believed that nisser have pointed heads, but no one has ever known for sure. It's our secret, and we keep it under our hats!"

"I don't have any secrets," Erik said wistfully, "except that I like Jenny."

Nils laughed and said, "That's no secret! Why don't you let *me* be your secret?"

"Hey, that's a neat idea! But how are we going to work it? Mrs. Anderson nearly caught me talking to you after school, and my folks are sure to notice."

Nils picked up the earphones of a portable radio. "How about these? Put them on."

Erik did and heard Nils say, "Testing, station NISSE broadcasting at one million megahertz. Do you hear me?"

"Loud and clear! But how will I talk to you?"

"Just send me a thought. I'll pick it up."

"You mean you can read my mind?"

"Not all of it—just what's meant for me. After all, no decent nisse would read somebody else's mail, and I don't pry into private thoughts, either."

Erik decided to test the system, thinking, "Nils, where do you want to sleep?"

The answer came through the earphones. "How about one of those drawers?"

Erik opened the sock drawer, and Nils took a look.

"Too lumpy," he said.

The underwear drawer was such a jumble that Erik was

embarrassed to suggest it. Besides, it had hard stuff like a pocket knife, a toy truck and an action figure dumped into it.

"Try the bottom drawer," said Nils.

Sweatshirts would make a fine bed, they both decided, and Nils climbed into the drawer to try it out. He snuggled down in the soft, knitted shirts and smiled contentedly.

A door slammed somewhere in the house, and Erik said, "My dad is home. You'd better get invisible."

Nils disappeared with another fingersnap, and sure enough, Jon Dahl rapped on the bedroom door and opened it without waiting for an invitation.

"Hi, Dad!" Erik said.

"What kind of a day did you have?"

"It was OK."

"Didn't your class go to the museum today? Somebody at Kiwanis said the fifth graders were supposed to be there."

"Yeah, we went."

"We had to go when I was a kid. They've made it a lot more interesting now than it was then."

"It was pretty interesting, all right," Erik said.

"Ever think about scooping out this room?"

"Dad!" Erik groaned.

"OK, OK! Your mother wants you to wash your hands for dinner."

As Erik's father left the room, toys, books and clothes began to fly through the air and come down stacked, folded and hung away.

"Wow!" said Erik, "I forgot what color my rug was. It's blue!"

Nils chuckled.

"Erik," his mother called. "Dinner is served."

"What are we having?"

"Pizza and salad."

Erik asked Nils if he liked pizza.

"Never had any," came the answer on the earphones.

Erik went to the table in the dining room and pulled an extra dining chair next to his.

"What's that for?" his mother asked.

Erik nearly panicked. He had no good explanation for Nils's chair, but he had to say something. "I just wanted to see what it would feel like to have another person in the family," he said.

His father and mother exchanged a long, meaningful look.

"What's with the earphones?" his father asked.

Again, Erik nearly panicked, but he said, "There's a program I really want to hear."

"Well, let's turn on the big radio and we'll all listen," said his father.

"Oh, no, Dad! It's something you'd hate—a group called the Nisser."

His father winced. "Heavy metal, I suppose. After the day I put in at the bank, that's all I need. You're on your own, Erik!"

"Really, Jon," his mother said. "Wearing earphones at the table is terribly rude."

"Please, Mom! I really want to hear this!"

"Oh, all right."

Erik's mother put a big wedge of pizza on his plate and sighed. "I suppose you won't eat all of this. You pick at your food like a bird!"

Nils spoke into the earphones. "I don't see a fork for me."

Erik thought, "I'll pretend to drop this one. You catch it, and I'll get another one from the drawer."

Erik's parents talked to each other. His mother told about the couple that wanted to buy a house she listed but couldn't get financing. His father told about refusing a loan to some other people who would never pay it back.

They weren't looking at Erik, so they failed to see two forks at work on his pizza. One flew in a blur and the other lifted a bite now and then. When the plate was empty, the forks attacked the salad, spearing tomatoes and lettuce with lightning speed.

"Whatever this is, I like it," said Nils through the earphones.

"It's pizza," Erik thought. "It comes from Italy."

"No wonder I never had any!" Nils responded.

Erik's mother saw that his food was gone and couldn't believe it. "I just said you eat like a bird," she said.

"More like a vulture!" said his father.

"May I have more, please?" Erik asked.

"Will wonders never cease!" said his mother.

"If you keep going like this, maybe you'll grow enough to—"

"Jon," his mother said, "forget the jock stuff. Let's just be glad that he's eating decently for a change."

Then it was time for ice cream, and Erik managed to drop his spoon. His mother brought him another immediately. Nils loved Goo-Goo Cluster ice cream.

That night when Nils settled down among the sweatshirts, he said, "I think I'm going to like it here— now that we've got the place cleaned up. Good-night, Erik."

"Good-night, Nils." Erik lay awake for a long time thinking about his remarkable day. He hadn't turned on the television at all because he was too busy living.

Nils Makes the Team

Erik's mother was surprised to see her son eating a bowl of oatmeal for breakfast and asking for two slices of toast. Usually, she was lucky if she could get him to eat a small serving of a cold cereal.

He dropped his spoon, saying, "Oops! Guess I'd better get a clean one."

"Erik, I've never known you to be so clumsy," she said. "Not since you were in your highchair!" But she smiled when she said it.

His father lowered the newspaper to grin at him, too, and said, "At least we can't complain about your appetite."

They both went back to their newspapers, allowing Nils to dig into the cereal bowl with gusto and chomp down a piece of toast in seconds.

"Mom," Erik said, "Jenny asked me to her birthday party tonight after school. Will you get her a present?"

"*Now* you tell me!" his mother said with a groan. "I have two houses to show and a luncheon meeting today."

"OK, OK, so I won't give her a present," Erik said. "Maybe I won't even go."

He looked so sad that Nils sent him an earphone message, "I'll get a present for Jenny."

But Erik's mother said, "Don't worry about it, Honey. I'll find the time somewhere. I'll wrap it and put it on the hall table."

His father said, "Are those earphones permanently attached to your head? You'd think we were having breakfast with an alien!"

Nils sent a quick message, a laugh followed by, "That's exactly what they're doing!"

"Wow," Erik said, "it's later than I thought. I have gym first period, and I have to change. 'Bye!"

"Please excuse yourself from the table," his mother said.

"Excuse me." Erik grabbed his jacket, thought, "Come on, Nils," and dashed out the back door. He started to take his fifth alternative route, then remembered that he didn't need it. He and Nils arrived at the school five minutes early.

They went into Mrs. Anderson's room for roll call and announcements and then hurried to the boys' locker room.

"Bring your ladder today, Erik?" Bobby taunted.

"How would you like your fingers stuck together permanently?" Erik said. "Remember what happened yesterday?"

"Aw, I was just kidding," Bobby said.

Erik put on his orange satin shorts, his white T-shirt and his hightops, feeling less confident than he looked.

Mr. Rolf, the gym teacher, was bouncing the ball under the hoop when Erik came into the gym, and he threw it in Erik's direction.

Much to Erik's surprise, the ball turned a corner in the air and came straight into his hands.

"Nice catch!" Mr. Rolf said, amazed. "Come over and try some baskets."

Erik walked to the free throw line and looked up at the hoop. It seemed a million miles away, but he took a deep breath, pulled back and let the ball fly. It bounced off the rim, and even without the earphones, he got a faint message from Nils: "Don't get excited. We have to work into this gradually, or they won't believe it."

Erik reclaimed the ball and laid it up again, thinking, "Nils, I really want this one."

This time, the ball soared and dropped cleanly through the hoop with a whisper of nothing but net.

"Well, I'll be!" said Mr. Rolf.

Bobby and the other big guys were just standing there with their mouths open.

"OK, let's play ball!" Mr. Rolf shouted.

Usually, this was Erik's signal to head for the sidelines, but when he started toward the bench, they all protested. He found himself running, dribbling and shooting with everyone cheering, and he'd never been happier.

At the end of the period, Mr. Rolf said, "I don't know what fired you up, but whatever it is, keep it going. Welcome to the team. Go on in there and choose a jersey number."

Erik thought, "You choose the number, Nils. You're doing all the playing."

Without earphones, the reception was terrible, but he made out what Nils was saying: "Make it number nine. The ancient Norse believed in nine worlds, and I've always thought that was a good, round number."

Erik showered, and nobody noticed that an invisible hand offered him his towel. The room was too steamy to see such things.

He told the coach he'd take number nine, and then he remembered that was Bobby's number.

"Do you really feel strongly about that number?" Mr. Rolf said.

"It's that or nothing," Erik said.

"OK, I'll talk to Bobby."

As Erik walked away, Nils waited long enough to hear Mr. Rolf tell another teacher, "I can't believe what's happened to Erik Dahl. I always thought he was a wimp, but today he was hotter than a pistol on that court. If he wants number nine, Bobby Helms will just have to give it up."

Erik was walking down the hall, thinking a message to Nils, "How did you get so good if you never played before?"

"I used to watch Thor throw his hammer. He could split mountains with that thing!"

"Thor?"

"The thunder god, Odin's son. He used to drive a chariot pulled by goats. He had a red beard, blue eyes, and the best aim in Asgard."

"Asgard?"

"That was the fortress of the gods many ages ago. I'll tell you all about it some other time. Right now, you have to get to class, or you'll get detention during Jenny's birthday party."

22

The day passed quickly. Erik tried very hard to do well in all his subjects because he wanted Nils to see him at his best.

In the lunchroom at noon, Erik took double spoons and forks. He usually asked the woman behind the counter to give him less than the others got, but today, he asked for more. Was she ever surprised!

"Are you in a growing spurt?" she asked. "Good for you!"

His tray held two hotdogs, a mound of canned corn, two peanut butter sandwiches, and some Tater Tots plus two big brownies. Erik also picked up two cartons of milk and two straws.

The problem now was to find a place for Nils on the long bench. Kids were always sliding up and down, bumping into each other and yelling and screaming—until the teachers came and made them stop.

With all the noise, Erik had to concentrate harder than ever to pick up Nils's message: "I'll just sit cross-legged in the middle of the table. Try to keep a space clear in front of your tray."

Earphones were not allowed in school, and Erik grew so tired from heavy concentrating that he decided to send Nils a thought message that he'd be off the air for awhile.

Nils responded with a faint, "Just a minute. Better wish Jenny a happy birthday."

"Can't I do that when I get to the party?"

"You can do it again then. It's impossible to pay too much attention to girls."

The double forks and spoons had cleaned Erik's tray, and he had very little to dump into the trash barrel when he returned his dishes. He knew that he had eaten more than usual, and it made him feel good.

He stopped behind Jenny, who was sitting with her friends, and tugged at her braid gently. This time, he needed no help from Nils.

"What do *you* want?" she said in a sassy voice.

"Just wanted to wish you a happy birthday," Erik said. "See you later."

Nils commented, "She reminds me of Sif, Thor's wife. Loki cut off Sif's beautiful, blonde hair while she was asleep, and the dwarf goldsmiths replaced it with fine strands of real gold."

"Who was Loki?"

"He was a half-god who was beautiful but evil—the master of cunning. His father was the wind giant. I could tell you tales of Loki for years on end, but we don't have time today."

After school, Erik and Nils raced home, using the most direct route. They saw Bobby and his friends lurking, but today, they were only looking. They were afraid to beat up on Erik now.

On the hall table was a lovely package with a pink ribbon and a tag that read "To Jenny from Erik."

Nobody was at home, so Erik spoke to Nils aloud. "I wish I knew what was in that box. I hate to be surprised about what I'm giving. What if she doesn't like it?"

"Your mother probably knows what girls like," Nils said. "After all, she was one not so very long ago."

"Things were different then," Erik said.

Nils laughed and said, "I guess you have to be around a few centuries before you realize that some things never change."

"Here's a note on the refrigerator door," Erik called from the kitchen. "It says, 'Have a cola but nothing else. You'll have plenty of sweets at the party.'"

"What's a cola?" Nils asked.

"It's a sweet, fizzy brown drink," said Erik, reaching for a glass. "I'll pour you some."

Nils tried it and smiled broadly. "This tastes even better than the goat's milk of Valhalla," he said.

"What's Valhalla?" Erik asked.

"The heaven where great warriors go."

"Warriors probably would like cola," Erik said.

"So would the gods," said Nils.

"Well, I guess we have to get cleaned up for the party. I'll have to change my pants and put on a clean shirt. Don't you ever change your clothes?"

"These are self-renewing threads," said Nils. "The norns wove my first suit from magic yarn, and when it wears a bit thin, it remakes itself."

"But don't you get dirty?"

"Absolutely not! Dirt stops at a barrier a millimeter from my person. It never touches me or my clothing. And the thing we nisser pride ourselves upon the most is our wonderful scent. We smell like sunlight, gardens and ocean breezes. It's just the way we are."

"Lucky you! I smell like old gym shoes most of the time—even after I take a bath."

"Well, get on with it!" Nils said. "The party starts in half an hour."

Erik started toward his room, then turned and said, "Do you really think that present will be OK?"

"If you insist, I can tell you what's in it."

"Naw, that's OK."

Jenny answered the door wearing a pink dress that matched the bow on Erik's present. How could his mom be so smart, he wondered?

The answer came through the earphones, "I sent your mother a nissegram. People never know why, but suddenly a thought is there, and they go with it."

Erik wished Jenny a happy birthday for the second time and went inside, closely followed by Nils.

"Why are you wearing those earphones?" Jenny asked.

"I'm listening for an important announcement," Erik said with an extremely serious expression.

"Oh! Well, come on in. We're getting ready to play a game."

The other kids were milling around in their best clothes, staring at the table piled with presents. Some of them waved at Erik and others didn't, but he got a better response than he usually did.

Jenny's mother announced a game of Pin the Tail on the Donkey, and one of the boys groaned. Amy volunteered to be blind-folded first. Jenny's mother turned her around and around until she almost fell down dizzy. Then Amy pinned the tail on the donkey's ear.

25

Others tried and failed to do much better, and then it was Erik's turn. The room went round and round when he stopped turning, and he felt the grip of nisse fingers guiding his own as he approached the donkey. The next thing he heard was clapping. Pulling off the blindfold, he saw the tail perfectly placed.

"Isn't that overdoing it a bit, Nils?" he thought.

Just then Jenny said, "Maybe somebody told him how to do it over those earphones."

Erik shook his head violently. "No! There's nothing to hear! See for yourself!" He ripped the earphones off and held them out to anyone who wanted to check. No one did.

They played more games, and then it was time to cut the cake. The lovely, tall, pink cake was blazing with eleven candles.

Jenny blew and blew, but one candle kept coming back. Nils told Erik, "That looks like the work of Loki, the fire god."

"No," Erik thought. "It's a trick candle. The only way you can put it out is to dump it into water."

Jenny was nearly ready to cry. If she couldn't blow out the candles with one breath, she wouldn't get her wish.

Suddenly, the offending candle lifted itself from the cake and floated out of the room. The sound of running water could be heard in the distance.

"I don't believe what I just saw!" said Jenny's mother.

Nils told Erik, "Tell her that planning a birthday party is pretty exhausting. She probably *didn't* see what she doesn't believe."

Erik did as he was told, and Jenny's mother looked at him with amazement. "You certainly are mature for a fifth grader, Erik. You're probably right."

They went into the living room to open the presents, and when Jenny untied the pink bow on Erik's box and looked inside, she gasped with delight.

"I got my wish!" she said, lifting out a golden clasp for her braid that would make her look like a princess. "How could you ever know?"

"I have some friends who seem to know everything," said Erik, giving her braid a gentle tug. She punched him in the upper arm to show her gratitude, and they parted on good terms.

On the way home, Erik asked Nils, "Who were the norns? The ones who wove your clothes?"

"Actually, they wove people's lives, deciding the fate of every person ever born. They did clothes for nisser on the side. Their names were Urd, Verdande and Skuld, and even the high gods bowed to their decisions. They lived at the foot of the World Tree near the Fountain of Wisdom. The norns wove our meeting, Erik, and I'm glad."

"So am I!" said Erik.

Nils's History Lesson

Erik walked home from school slowly, scuffing the toes of his hightops. Nils walked beside him invisibly, and since nobody was around, he asked, "What's the matter, Erik?"

Erik sighed and said, "It's that paper I have to write. Old Lady Anderson wants it tomorrow, and I haven't even started."

"What's it about?" Nils asked.

"How we got our Constitution," Erik said gloomily. "I can't get into it."

They went into the house and straight to the refrigerator. Erik's mother had left a note on the door that said, "Drink juice! It's good for you!"

Erik poured orange juice into two glasses, which they took to the family room. Nils jumped to the arm of the sofa and swung his shiny, black boots over the edge. Erik scootched back in his father's lounge chair until his legs stuck straight out in front of him.

"Why do you call her 'Old Lady Anderson'?" Nils asked. "She doesn't look very old to me."

"Hey, man, she's old!" Erik said. "Probably about twenty-six."

Nils laughed and said, "The most beautiful woman I've ever seen is thousands of years old!"

"Yeah? Who is she?"

"Freyja, the goddess of beauty. When she cries, the tears are pure gold."

"What does she have to cry about?" Erik asked.

"Her husband took off. She wanted this necklace of diamonds and gold, see? But she had to ask these three giant women if she could have it. Her husband told her he didn't want her hanging around the giants, and when he saw that necklace, he knew she had visited them."

Erik said, "My dad doesn't tell my mom what to do."

Nils shrugged. "I guess things are different now."

They finished their juice and put the glasses in the kitchen sink. Nils handed his to Erik because he couldn't reach that high.

"Why don't you start your paper?" Nils suggested.

"I can't think of anything to say, and I don't feel like going to the library."

"Where did all this happen—this Constitution thing?"

"Philadelphia."

"Have you ever been there?"

"No. If I had, this would be easier."

"Let's go, then!" Nils said, leaping toward the door.

Erik laughed. "It's not just down the street, Nils. It's hundreds of miles away."

"That's no problem. I can borrow Thor's chariot. It's pulled by goats."

"Goats?" Erik said doubtfully.

"Well, if you don't like goats, I think I can get Freyja's chariot pulled by big, white cats. Would you prefer the cats?"

"Now just a minute," Erik said. "My folks would never let me do that. Besides, it would take days, and my paper is due tomorrow."

"No problem," said Nils. "I'll put the hour we're in on hold. Your folks won't get home from work before we get back. And the trip won't take long. Those cats really take off!"

"OK, let's go!" said Erik, grabbing his hooded jacket.

"Just go outside and wait for me at the curb," Nils said. "I have to send a nisse fax to Freyja. It may take a few minutes, because she often turns into a falcon and flies off around this time of day."

As Erik rushed out of the house, Nils called after him, "You're not allergic to cats, are you?"

"Nope."

Erik waited, looking up and down the street nervously. He hoped none of the neighbors would look out their windows and see this chariot Nils was ordering. The UPS truck pulled up to the house next door to deliver a package.

"Hurry up and get out of here!" Erik said under his breath.

The brown truck drove away, and suddenly the chariot was right there with Nils holding the long strands of pearls that were the reins. The big, fluffy, white cats were the size of Shetland ponies. Eight of them were hitched to the chariot.

"Get in!" said Nils.

Erik opened the white velvet door with a diamond handle and sat beside Nils on a fat, white velvet cushion. The cats stretched out like flying squirrels.

"I think you made the right choice," said Nils. "Thor's chariot smells like goats, now that I think of it."

He had scarcely finished his sentence when the chariot glided to a stop in front of a red brick building with a white clock tower. Horse-drawn buggies were coming and going, and people were getting out to enter the building.

"This is the right place, I hope," Nils said.

Erik heard a guide say, "Ladies and gentlemen, you see before you Independence Hall."

"Yeah," he said in amazement. "How did you know how to get here?"

"That's easy," Nils said. "NTT."

"What does that mean?"

"Nisse Travel Treats. The agency's motto is 'Nothing too tough!' Shall we go inside?"

"What about—" Erik pointed to the cats, who were looking around with their slanty blue eyes, and waving their plume-like tails back and forth.

Nils draped the pearl reins over the sapphire windshield and waved at the cats. They disappeared, along with the chariot, and Nils said he'd better disappear too.

"Did you bring your earphones?" he asked Erik. "If I'm going to help you, I want the reception to be clear."

"I forgot!"

"Oh well, nobody will notice that my voice is coming from nowhere. If they think it's odd, what do we care? We don't know anybody around here anyhow."

They joined a group of tourists and went inside, making their way to the Assembly Room.

The guide pointed and said, "Here at this simple, wooden desk, James Madison wrote down the proceedings of the Constitutional Congress with a quill made from a crow's feather."

"Neat!" thought Erik.

Nils said, "They signed it September 17, 1787. Remember that date!"

A woman tourist looked around angrily and said, "I'm not taking a test on this trip, am I?"

"Pardon me, Madame," said Nils, "I was speaking to someone else."

She fixed her eyes where she thought the speaker should be, saw nothing, and moved quickly to another part of the room.

The guide said, "As the Constitution was being signed, Benjamin Franklin said, 'The chair of the president is carved with a rising sun, not a setting one.' "

Nils asked Erik, "Are you starting to get into it?"

Erik nodded.

They went out into the street, and Nils consulted NTT to learn of the other attractions. They went to the house of Betsy Ross, where a flag with thirteen stars flew from a high window, and paid their respects to the Liberty Bell.

"I know a gnome who could fix that crack in nothing flat," Nils said.

"Yeah, but that would kind of spoil it," Erik said.

"Have you seen enough?"

"Why, do we have to get back?"

"Well, Freyja always has been generous with me, and I don't like to push her generosity too far."

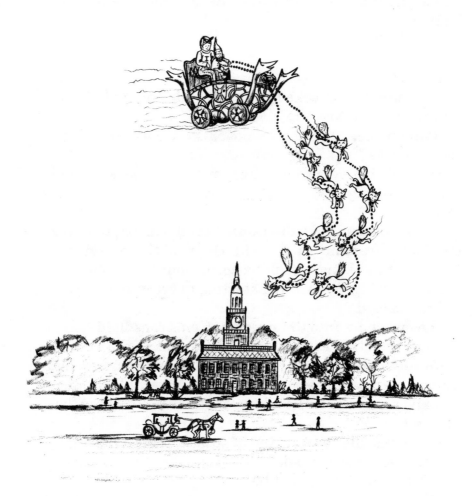

*Nils, Erik, the chariot and the cats coming in for a landing
at Independence Hall.*

A horse-drawn buggy stopped near them, and the guide told the tourists, "Philadelphia, the City of Brotherly Love, is the birthplace of our nation."

Nils guided Erik down a side street, where their cat-drawn chariot materialized in all its dazzling beauty. As they climbed in, they noticed a scuffle across the street. One man was robbing another.

Nils, now visible, scratched his beard in puzzlement. "How can that happen in the City of Brotherly Love?"

"Do something, Nils!" Erik urged.

The next thing Erik saw was a wallet flying from the thief's pocket and making its way back to its owner's hands. The thief was running away, holding his hands to his face and howling with pain.

Nils jumped into the chariot, took up the pearly reins, and gave a Norwegian command to the cats. They were above cloud cover before Erik could look back at Independence Hall.

"What did you do to that guy?" Erik asked.

"Just pinched his nose a bit. When you pinch other people's money, that's what you deserve."

They were home by 3:20, which was just about the time they left. Erik got out of the chariot and started to stroke one of the chariot cats, but they vanished. He was stroking air.

"Now can you write that paper?" Nils asked.

"I can try," said Erik.

"Good! While you're doing that, I'll have another can of pop. Starting a nation is thirsty work!"

Erik wrote about the wooden desk, the crow quill pen, the chair with the rising sun, and the seven weeks of talk to get the Constitution right.

Old Lady Anderson said, "This is really good, Erik. You must have done a lot of research on Philadelphia."

"Yeah," said Erik, "I really did, but I had to cover a lot of ground in a hurry."

And he thought, "Thanks for the ride, Nils. Tell your friend Freyja that flight was first class!"

Because he couldn't wear the earphones in school, he didn't hear Nils's reply. "I sent a can of pop back with the carriage—a little thank-you gift."

Nils Visits Little Norway

One morning when Nils yawned and climbed out of the sweatshirt drawer, Erik decided that he looked sad.

"Are you homesick?" Erik asked. "*I* was when I went to camp last summer."

Nils straightened his hat and admitted that he *was* a bit homesick. "Norway is so beautiful! High, snowy mountains—wooden churches with dragon heads, bright houses, long fjords with water as still as a mirror. Not that it isn't nice around here, Erik, but I do miss all that."

"I don't want you to leave," Erik said, "so I'll have to think of something."

All through breakfast, Erik thought and thought. His mother asked him why he was so quiet, and he told her he was trying to figure something out.

"Maybe we can help," his father suggested.

"Well," Erik said, "it's supposed to look like Norway around here, but we don't have any mountains with snow—or any fjords. I'd sure like to see something like that."

"Someday you will," his father said.

"I mean sooner than someday," said Erik.

His mother said, "Tomorrow is Saturday, and we could drive up to Little Norway. You won't see mountains with snow or fjords, but they have a stave church and some log houses."

"That would be neat!" Erik said.

His father said, "I really ought to work."

"Then I'll take him," his mother said.

"Oh, what the heck! Let's all go!"

The next morning, Erik awoke very early and packed a knapsack of apples and cookies for the trip. When his parents finally got up, he was all dressed and ready to go.

They always had kringle for breakfast on weekends, a real

treat after eating porridge all week, but today, Erik was too impatient to enjoy it.

"Let's go!" he urged.

"Don't get excited, Son," his father said. "Nissedahle will wait for us."

Erik felt a tug at his sleeve, a reminder that he hadn't put on his earphones. He grabbed them from the kitchen counter.

"Erik!" his mother said, "Must you?"

He nodded and heard Nils say, "Nissedahle? You mean the nisser will be there?"

Erik thought, "Just a minute, Nils, I'll try to find out." He said aloud, "Why do they call it that? I thought it was Little Norway."

His father explained, "A Chicago man named Isak Dahle bought the place for a summer home a long time ago, and he called it Valley of the Elves. He changed the Norwegian spelling to make it like his name."

"Oh," said Erik. "Do they have nisser there?"

"My goodness, Erik," his mother said, "I didn't realize you knew that word. You must have learned it when you visited Vesterheim."

"Yeah, I guess," said Erik. "Well, do they?"

"I doubt it," she said. "I've never seen any."

Erik sent a thought message to Nils. "You heard what she said. I suppose you're disappointed."

Nils sighed. "I *did* think I might run into some distant relatives. But just because humans haven't seen them doesn't mean they're not there."

"We'll soon find out," said Erik. "Let's get in the car."

Nils said, "I've never ridden in a car."

"Then I'd better tell you that you have to fasten your seat belt."

They went outside, Erik carrying his knapsack. Erik got into the back seat, and his father nearly shut the door on Nils.

"Wait!" Erik yelled, sticking out his leg to hold it open.

"What now?" his father said.

Feeling a tap on his shoulder that told him Nils was safely inside, he said, "Nothing. Let's go."

They drove out of town toward the Mississippi River, and Erik saw a moving bulge in his knapsack. Nils was helping himself to an apple. Fortunately, Erik's parents didn't notice the apple suspended in the air with nisse bites turning red skin to white flesh.

Nils said, "The cat chariot would be faster."

"Yeah," Erik thought, "but my folks would freak out if they saw that!"

When they came to the river and crossed the high bridge to Prairie du Chien, Erik thought, "Do you have a river like that in Norway?"

"Can't say that we do," Nils answered, dumping his apple core into Erik's hand. Erik put it in the trash bag.

Before arriving at Little Norway, which is near Blue Mounds, Wisconsin, they stopped for a hamburger, and Erik's parents were surprised when he asked for two, but they ordered them. French fries, too. Nils was crazy about the French fries.

Guides in Norwegian dress were waiting to conduct tours of the barn, the granary, the family home, the bachelor's cabin, the sod-roofed cottage and the stave church. Erik's parents paid the admission and joined a group of visitors.

Erik went to stand beside them. His mother told him to take off his earphones so he could hear the guide. She told about Osten Olson Haugen, a carpenter and stonemason from Telemark in Norway, who settled here in 1856. Their house was still standing.

Suddenly Erik had the feeling that Nils was not with him.

"Nils?" he thought. "Where are you?"

His mother frowned when she saw him put the earphones on again.

Nils said, "Over here—near the church. Come on over!"

"Please, Mom," Erik said, "I want to see the church before all these people get in the way. I won't get lost."

"No, you'd better stay with us," she said.

"Let him go, Sonja," his father said.

Erik ran toward the church, which was reflected in a quiet pond. Its dragon heads pointed to the sky from the layered peaks of the roof.

"Up here!" said Nils. "I'm just checking out the carving. It's a pretty good replica of 12th century work."

"Who made it?" Erik thought.

Nils answered, "I'm not sure who, but I know when. They did it for the Columbian Exposition in Chicago in 1893. Phillip Wrigley, the chewing gum man, gave it to Little Norway in 1935."

"I'm going in," Erik said, but the door was locked. Suddenly it wasn't locked and he stepped inside.

He could feel that Nils was beside him as he looked at a piece of a Viking ship and an old piece of music written by somebody called Edvard Grieg.

"I knew Grieg personally," Nils said. "I'll tell you about it sometime."

They went to explore the stabbur, a storage house on raised foundations, and then on to the other buildings. Erik really liked the six-legged rocking chair.

They nearly created a riot when Nils blew on the lur, a big horn the Norwegians used to send messages in the mountains. All the guides came running to see who had touched this wonderful antique, and Erik had the wit to get away from it so he couldn't be blamed.

Nils led him to the mountain hut and helped him climb up to sit on the grass that grew from the sod roof. They chose the side that faced the woods so nobody could see them. Now and then they climbed up and peeked over the ridge of the roof.

"I couldn't resist trying that lur," Nils said. "I remember when a young girl named Prillar-Guri blew it to warn the people in all the valleys that the Scots were coming."

"When was that?" Erik asked.

Nils blows a high note on the lur

"Sometime in the 17th century, I think. That girl had a fine pair of lungs!"

"You look a lot happier than you did yesterday," Erik said.

"I am!" said Nils. "Just sitting here on the roof looking at the buildings against the hills and the church reflected in the pond makes me think I've found a bit of home."

They watched the group of visitors move from one building to the next. Erik's mother was looking about anxiously.

"Why don't you join them?" Nils said. "I'll stay here and give those people a treat."

"What are you going to do?"

"I'm going to make myself visible and stand up on this roof. When you come to Nissedahle, you really should see a nisse, don't you think?"

"It sounds risky to me. What if somebody tries to grab you?"

"They won't," Nils said. "They'll never believe I'm real. Go on, now."

Erik inched down the sod roof and jumped from the eaves of the low mountain hut. As he came into view, his mother waved and motioned for him to join them.

"You missed the spring house," she said.

Nils on top of the sod roof.

Erik turned back to the mountain hut, saw Nils straddling the peak of the roof with his hands on his hips and yelled, "Look! A nisse!"

"That wasn't here the last time I came," one woman said. "Isn't it adorable?"

"It must be a little kid dressed up like an elf," her husband said.

"It's not moving. It must be carved. That's it, a carved nisse."

"I want one, Mommy!" a little girl said. "I want a nisse!"

"Maybe they have some in the gift shop."

Erik sent a thought message to Nils. "If you move, it will ruin everything. You're going to have to stand there forever."

Nils answered through the earphones. "I can stand still as long as I have to. I won't move a muscle."

The guide was moving toward the mountain hut now, and the group followed her. People were asking her about the carved nisse, and she didn't know what to say.

Finally, she said, "I don't know how it got there. It wasn't

40

there this morning. I'll have to ask the manager about it."

The group stood looking up at Nils, and the guide said uncertainly, "There's something different about that nisse."

"I'm surprised you don't have more of them," one of the women said. "It really adds a lot to the place."

Erik thought, "How are we going to get you off that roof, Nils?"

Nils said, "Distract the guide."

Erik caught her attention and asked, "How do you know so much about nisser?"

"Young man," she said, "I am a student of Norwegian folklore, and I'm really annoyed that I wasn't informed about this new figure in time to add information about it to my remarks."

"Did you ever see a real nisse around here?" Erik asked.

"Erik, for heaven's sake!" his mother said, frowning.

The guide realized the other visitors were getting impatient. She said, "Now if you'll come with me, I'll show you the dugout where the Haugens spent their first winter in this valley in 1856."

"Well, Erik," his father said, "you missed most of the tour, and you were the one who wanted to come here."

"That's OK, Dad, I saw a lot of neat stuff."

They moved on, and when Erik looked back, Nils still straddled the roof peak, hands on his hips. He was smiling.

Erik sent him a thought. "See you in the car."

Erik and his parents considered how miserable it would be to live in a hole in the ground in the winter and went on to look at round hope chests for storing lace, ale bowls, and chairs with rosemaling.

The next time Erik had a chance to glance at the mountain hut, Nils was gone from the roof. Then Erik realized that the car was locked. He wasn't sure how far his thought message would travel, but he tried. "You can't get in until Dad brings the key. Wait for us."

Nils answered immediately. "Who needs keys? I'm in the back seat eating cookies."

When they were ready to go home, Erik's father said, "Did you have a good time?"

Erik nodded. He was tired.

"What did you like best?"

Erik chuckled and said, "The nisse on the roof."

"You certainly pestered the guide about that," his mother said. "You almost acted as if you knew more than she does, and she has studied these things."

Erik repeated something he'd heard his mother say quite often, "Sometimes it's who you know."

"*Whom* you know," she corrected.

"Whatever," Erik said, resting his head on Nils's sturdy, little shoulder and drifting toward sleep.

"I hope you're not as homesick now," he thought. "You'll stay?"

"I'll stay," Nils answered, brushing the cookie crumbs out of his beard.

Nils Goes to Florida

One day when Erik and Nils were drinking apple juice after school, Erik's mother rushed in so fast that Nils barely had time to make himself invisible.

"That was close!" Erik thought.

"Too close!" came Nils's reply through the earphones. "I'm starting to feel so much at home here that I'm getting careless!"

"Erik," his mother said, "take off those earphones and listen to me! I have wonderful news!"

"I'm off the air again," he thought. He pulled the earphones off and said, "What, Mom?"

"I sold the Grant house—the big one on the hill! The commission will be terrific!"

"Great!" said Erik, raising his glass in a toast to her success. He hoped she wouldn't notice the second glass that belonged to Nils.

"I'm going to call your father right now and tell him!"

She got on the phone, and Erik could hear how pleased his father was. He thought about turning on the television, but something she said made him forget all about that.

"Jon, what do you think about taking Erik to Walt Disney World right after Christmas? My commission ought to cover it."

"Yay!" Erik shouted.

His mother smiled and put her finger to her lips because she couldn't hear what his father was saying.

Then her expression changed. "That's right, we probably couldn't get airplane reservations this late. Well, it was a nice idea."

"Mom," Erik said urgently, pulling at her arm. "Couldn't we borrow Grandpa's RV?"

"There's a thought!" she said, relaying it to his father.

Erik felt a tug at his sleeve, a reminder to put the earphones on.

Nils told him, "I don't know what an RV is, but if that doesn't work, we can always use NTT—nothing too tough."

"Yeah, all right!" Erik thought. Then he explained to Nils, "An RV is a recreational vehicle, sort of like a little house on wheels. You can sleep in it and eat in it and everything."

"It must be bigger than the car," Nils said.

"Oh, lots bigger."

Grandma and Grandpa Dahl usually went off to some warm place in the RV themselves, but this year, they wanted to stay in Decorah until after their wedding anniversary in February. They were happy to lend the RV to their son and his family. Erik was sure they would have been happy to let a nisse travel in it, too, if they had known. Grandma Dahl always put a carved nisse on her mantel at Christmas time. She liked nisser, and Erik supposed that Grandpa Dahl liked them, too.

They were so busy planning their trip that they sailed right through Christmas without feeling the usual rush. When his father had made the Christmas tree secure in its stand, Erik started to decorate it. With Nils's help, it was fast work. Garlanded with red yarn and bright with painted wood cut-outs, it was gorgeous.

As they were working, Erik's mother said, "I'm surprised that you haven't asked for anything special for Christmas. You always have *something* in mind."

Erik realized he had to think fast and said, "Well, I figured our trip was sort of a present."

His mother hugged him, saying, "You and your earphones!"

Nils said, "Your mother reminds me of Idun, the owner of the golden apples."

Erik thought, "You'll have to tell me about all those people on the way to Florida. We'll have plenty of time then."

"They're not exactly people," Nils said, "but I'll explain all that as we travel."

And he did. Not right away, however. Nils was so excited about the light, bright house on wheels that he had to explore every nook and cranny. Erik figured they'd be into Indiana before Nils settled down.

"What a great chariot!" Nils said. "Is it like the ship the dwarfsmiths made for Frey? When you get out, does it fold up and fit in your pocket?"

Erik laughed and thought, "No, it takes a pretty big parking space. Who's Frey?"

"He's the god of growth and harvest. He rules the elves who ripen grain and fruit, and rides a golden boar. He's Freyja's twin."

"Oh, yeah," thought Erik, "the owner of the cat carriage. And her brother rides a pig?"

Nils answered, "His name is Goldbristles, and his mane lights up the night."

"Are all these people—or whatever they are—still around? Old Lady Anderson says they're myths—not real. I thought she was right until I met you. *You're* real, and I rode in the cat chariot."

"Erik, human time moves on, and you can't go back. But anything or anyone you remember is still alive—in a way. Nisser time is different. We can move backward and forward, and our memory is better than yours. I can see the gods of Asgard as clearly as you see your mother and father, and we can talk with each other.

"Some people think it was all over after the Twilight of the Gods, but memory keeps it all alive. Do you understand?"

"I guess so," Erik thought doubtfully. "You mean that I could talk to Abraham Lincoln if I had a nisse memory?"

"Something like that."

"If you'll tell me what you remember, I'll get something for us to drink."

As Erik poured, Nils punched a cushion behind his back and made himself comfortable.

"I guess I'd better start at the beginning," Nils said.

"That's always a good idea," Erik thought with a chuckle.

Ymir the frost giant and the hornless ice cow

"Early in the morning of time, there was Niflheim, a place of frozen fog, and Muspelheim, a place of raging flames," Nils said. "And in between was a deep pit, Ginungagap. Finally, the fire and the ice whirled together and produced a frost giant named Ymir and a hornless ice cow."

Erik giggled and thought, "I know fat ladies eat ice milk instead of ice cream, but I never heard of an ice cow."

"Well," said Nils, "that's what Ymir lived on—the ice cow's milk. The cow licked the salty brim of the deep pit. Ymir fell into a deep sleep, and a male and a female jotun— that's giant, Erik—came to life in his left armpit."

Erik laughed and thought, "If they were giants, they probably were too heavy for the stork to bring."

"What sprouted from Ymir's feet was even worse! A troll with six heads!"

"Pretty ugly, huh?" Erik thought.

"Incredibly ugly! At any rate, the ice cow didn't think much of Ymir's production. She went on licking the brim of Ginungagap until a head of hair and a face appeared. This was a good-looking creature. His son was even better looking, and the son married a beautiful jotun maiden."

"From the armpit family?" Erik thought.

"That's right," said Nils. "This couple had three sons, Odin, Hoenir and Lodur. They were the first of the Aesir gods, and they represented Spirit, Will and Warmth.

"The three sons had the power to create a world, but first, they had to get rid of the frost giant. They killed him and pushed him into Ginungagap. The brine from his wounds overflowed the pit and drowned all the jotuns but one couple who escaped on an ice floe and lived on the wild outer shores of the sea formed from Ymir's brine."

Erik sipped and listened, fascinated by Nils's strange story. "And then what?" he thought.

"The Aesir raised Ymir's body from the sea and made earth from it. His flesh became the soil. His bones were the mountains, and his teeth were the stones and boulders. The gods pushed Niflheim down deep where it couldn't freeze the earth and set up Ymir's skull as the dome of the sky so sparks from flaming Muspelheim wouldn't set the new world on fire."

Erik's mother looked back at Erik and said to his father, "I expected him to ask, 'Are we almost there, yet?' before we left the city limits, but he hasn't said a word."

"You know, Sonja, we don't really know what he listens to on those earphones. Do you think we should monitor that?"

She laughed and said, "We'll get into the heavy parenting after the trip. Right now, I'm glad he's found something that keeps him occupied."

Nils had paused, politely, realizing that Erik needed to check out the conversation of his parents. Now he resumed his tale.

"The gods had placed a few sparks in the dome for sun, moon and stars, but there was no day or night because the sun and moon couldn't move."

"So what did they do," Erik thought, "get a battery?"

"Very funny," said Nils. "No, they made a cart for the sun and another for the moon and hitched up two teams of horses to trot them across the sky. The horses that pulled the moon had frosty manes, and the sun team had bellows strapped to their flanks to keep them from burning.

"Now, Erik, remember those jotuns who escaped on an ice floe and the six-headed troll?"

Erik nodded.

"These creatures hated the Aesir gods and their new world, and they hated light. They changed themselves into wolves and chased after the sun and the moon. Sometimes they caught them and ate them. But the sun and the moon disagreed with them, and they soon coughed them up again."

Erik giggled and thought, "You mean they barfed?"

"Well," said Nils primly, "yes, but I didn't want to sound gross. At any rate, once the Aesir gods had that much done, they created elves, gnomes, sprites, fish, birds, and animals. But something was missing."

"What?" thought Erik.

48

Ymir and a troll with six heads, plus two giants.

"They needed somebody to worship them, so they made humans. They saw two little trees, an ash and an alder, and they blew life into them. Odin gave them souls, Hoenir gave them the will to think and move, and Lodur gave them warm blood and feelings. The man's name was Ask (Ash) and the woman was called Embla (Alder), and their home, earth, was fenced by Ymir's eyebrows.

"As the generations went on, these crude creatures became smarter and better looking. They also had good manners, because Odin would disguise himself and visit them to teach them how to behave."

Erik's father asked, "Are you hungry? I see some golden arches just ahead."

Erik, who was still deep in Nils's story, didn't answer immediately—not until Nils punched him and said, "French fries! Let's go!"

Nils Visits Walt Disney World

Erik was so excited by the signs for the Magic Kingdom that he forgot to put his earphones on. He jumped up and down behind the driver's seat and yelled in his father's ear.

"Can't you go any faster, Dad?"

"Nope," his father said. "The traffic is too heavy. You'll just have to be patient."

"What are we going to do first?" Erik asked.

"Buy passports so we can get in," his mother said with a laugh.

They parked the RV, and as Erik was rushing to get out, he felt Nils tugging at his sleeve. He'd almost forgotten his earphones!

"It's winter," Nils said. "Why is it so warm?"

Erik shrugged, thinking, "That's just the way it is."

"I'll bet Loki has something to do with it," Nils said.

They boarded a tram to the Ticket and Transportation Center, and Erik thought, "Be careful where you sit, Nils. Somebody might squash you."

"I can take care of myself," Nils said.

They had to wait and wait to buy their passports because so many other people wanted to do the same thing.

Erik thought, "While we're standing around, why don't you tell me about this Loki character?"

"I guess the Magic Kingdom is a good place for that," Nils said. "Loki is a half-god. His father was the Wind Giant. He's what we call a shape changer."

"What's that?" Erik thought.

"He can be anything he wants to be. He turned himself into a mare and gave birth to Odin's eight-legged horse, Sleipnir. He turned himself into a fly and stung the eyelid

Loki

of the dwarf who was working on Thor's hammer. That's why it has a short handle."

Erik thought, "Didn't he get in trouble for that?"

"Did he ever!" Nils said. "Loki had made a bet that the dwarfsmiths working on the hammer couldn't do a better job than the ones who had made the gold hair for Sif, the folding ship for Frey, and Odin's great spear called Gungnir."

"What did he bet?" Erik thought.

"His head," Nils said. "The second team of dwarfsmiths made Frey's golden pig and Odin's great, golden ring called Draupnir—plus Thor's hammer. Loki lost his bet."

"So did they cut his head off?" Erik thought.

"No, because he said he hadn't bet his neck, and they couldn't touch that."

"Pretty smart!" Erik thought.

"Oh, Loki is nobody's dummy," said Nils. "But he did lose, so they sewed his lips shut with golden thread."

"Oooh!" Erik said aloud.

His parents looked at him in alarm, and he gave them a quick grin to prove that he was OK.

"We'll be on our way in a few minutes," his father promised, and so they were. They took the monorail to the Magic Kingdom.

Long lines of kids and their parents were everywhere, but the Dahls finally were walking on Main Street, U.S.A., enjoying the clip-clop sound made by horses pulling streetcars, and looking at the silent movie posters.

Nils had told Erik of his long sleep in the trunk, and now Erik thought, "This is about 1900. Is that when you came?"

"No," said Nils. "It was much earlier. They didn't have movies then."

Erik's mother said, "I can't believe you're wearing those earphones in a place like this. Do you want me to put them into my purse?"

"No, Mom, please!"

"Let's not argue about it," his father said. "He seems to be able to hear us well enough. Where shall we go now?"

Thor

Nils said, "I like the looks of that castle up there."

Erik pointed, and his father said, "Fantasyland?"

"Yeah."

They entered through Cinderella Castle and came upon Snow White and the Seven Dwarfs.

Nils said, "I don't recognize the girl, but the dwarfs look familiar—at least one of them does."

"Which one?" Erik thought.

"The one with the sour face."

"That's Grumpy," Erik thought. "And the girl is Snow White. She fell asleep for a long time, just the way you did."

"Interesting," said Nils. "She's quite pretty, once you get used to her unusual coloring. I've never seen a girl with such white, white skin and black, black hair."

Erik's mother said to his father, "Erik is very quiet. Do you think he's having a good time?"

"Of course he is, Sonja, but I'm surprised he chose Fantasyland first. I thought he'd be more interested in Tomorrowland."

His mother laughed and said, "We'll see to it that *you* get there, Jon."

As they walked on ahead, Nils suddenly became visible and skipped along beside Erik.

"Hey," Erik thought, "I can see you! Is that safe?"

"Sure," Nils said. "Everybody will think I work here. You can take your earphones off for awhile and we can have some normal conversation."

"Mom!" Erik called, "will you take my earphones?"

"Certainly," she said. "Who's your friend?"

"His name is Nils Nisse. He's from Norway."

The Dahls greeted Nils, thinking they were meeting him for the first time. Erik's father asked what part of Norway he came from, and Nils told him, "Not far from Kristiansund."

"Ah, that's on the west coast," said Erik's father.

Nils smiled and nodded.

"I think we'd better visit Tomorrowland if we want to keep your father happy, Erik."

They loved the race through Space Mountain and the ride on the *WEDway* PeopleMover. Nils danced up and down with delight.

Erik worried about Nils being without a passport, but he said he could always disappear if a problem arose.

In Liberty Square, Erik's mother suggested a steamboat trip, but Nils told Erik his last experience with a ship had not been pleasant. Instead, they went to hear Abraham Lincoln tell what America was all about.

Erik's parents were getting tired and wanted to go somewhere for a cup of coffee.

"Aw, do you *have* to?" Erik protested. "I want to go to Frontierland."

Nils tugged at Erik's sleeve, and when Erik's parents turned away from them, he whispered, "I'll put them on hold, and *we* can go."

"But Mom has my passport," Erik said. "What if I need it?"

"No problem," said Nils. The passport flew out of Mrs. Dahl's purse and into Erik's hand.

"Wow!" said Erik. "It's sure a good thing that you're honest."

Nils winked at him, and they were off.

The line for the Big Thunder Mountain Railroad runaway mine train was very, very long.

"We'll never get to the front of the line," Erik said with a deep sigh.

"I'll fix that," Nils said. He vanished right before Erik's eyes.

Suddenly, the line began to break up. Kids ran past Erik, and he moved up. Nils materialized beside him.

"What did you do?" Erik asked, amazed.

"Started a rumor that a dragon was loose on the train."

"Nobody would believe that!"

"Why not?" Nils said. "This is the Magic Kingdom, isn't it? Come on, let's go!"

The train took off with a roar, scattering a swarm of bats

and careening under a raging waterfall straight into an avalanche.

"Wow!" said Erik.

"Wow is right!" echoed Nils.

They listened to the country music of the electronically animated bears for awhile and decided to go on to Adventureland.

"Maybe I should check in with my folks first," Erik said. "They might get worried."

"I've taken care of that," Nils said.

"What did you do?"

"Put time on hold. The same thing I did when we went to Philadelphia."

They got into another long line, and while they waited, Nils told Erik about Loki's two wives, Sigunn and an ogress named Angerboda.

"Angerboda and Loki had two children," Nils said, "a spitting snake and a snapping wolf."

"That's weird!" said Erik.

Nils nodded. "They were so awful that even Odin couldn't kill them. He sent the snake to the bottom of the sea and put the wolf on an island in a lake surrounded by a forest of iron trees."

In no time at all, they were at the front of the line for the Jungle Cruise. Nils didn't seem to mind this boat, and they hung over the rail staring at the crocodiles, alligators and hippos in the water.

Nils was amazed at the apes, gorillas, lions and elephants along the shore.

"I've never seen anything like that!" he said.

"Of course you haven't," Erik said. "They live in warm places."

"Some of them look a lot like Loki's kids," Nils said with a chuckle.

The Swiss Family Treehouse with running water in all the rooms delighted Nils and Erik.

"They even have an organ!" Erik said. "In a tree! I'll bet

Odin sent the snake to the bottom of the sea.

58

we could build ourselves a tree house at home, Nils."

"What's the matter with the house you have?"

"Nothing," Erik said. "It would be fun to live in a tree, though."

They stopped to listen to the songs of the Enchanted Tiki Birds—more than two hundred of them—and as they walked on, Erik was singing "In The Tiki Tiki Tiki Tiki Tiki Room."

"That sure doesn't sound like Grieg," Nils said.

"Oh, yeah," Erik said, "you were going to tell me about that guy."

"Later. It's time that we found your parents."

Erik's father and mother had just ordered their coffee, and were turning to ask Erik what he and his friend wanted.

"Pop, I suppose," his father said.

"We saw a bunch of neat stuff!" Erik said.

Nils poked him, warning him not to say too much.

"Let's go to Epcot," Erik said.

"But you haven't seen all of the Magic Kingdom yet," his mother protested.

Nils poked him again, and Erik said, "What do *you* want to see, Mom?"

"Right now, I want to take a picture of you with your friend Nils."

"Oh, no!" said Nils.

"What's your problem?" Erik asked.

"Tell you later," Nils muttered, looking uncomfortable as Erik's mother positioned them with the castle in the background.

Then, after a family conference, they decided to get on the monorail for a fast ride to Epcot Center.

"Look at that thing!" Erik shouted, pointing at the gateway to Future World. "It looks like a giant golf ball!"

"It's a geosphere," his father said.

Nils stayed visible until the passports were needed. Then he disappeared and met them later.

They saw prehistoric beasts, which Nils said were very

much like some of the creatures of Norse mythology. They visited a space colony, and he said he'd never experienced anything like that.

Erik liked the floating ocean community, but Nils said he was afraid he'd get seasick living in a place like that.

Erik's mother was getting tired, and his father suggested that they go to the Norwegian Pavilion on the World Showcase Lagoon.

Nils was delighted with this bit of Norway, bright with rosemaling. He rushed up to a table of salmon, herring and all kinds of delicious Norwegian seafood, planning to help himself. Then he remembered that he had no money.

"Erik," he whispered, "will you lend me a couple of bucks?"

"Sure. Here you are."

Nils took it happily and found a waitress, a girl from Norway named Liv. They chatted in Norwegian, and although the place was crowded, Liv found a place to seat Nils and his friends.

Nils accompanied the Dahls to the hot table and to the cold table, recommending foods they would enjoy. When they had finished their meal, Nils gave Erik's father the money he had borrowed for his share of the bill.

"The North Sea Experience," Erik's mother read from a brochure. "Is that something you want to try?"

"Later," Nils said. "From what I know of the North Sea, this should not be done just after lunch."

"Well," she said, "we have several days here, so we can come back and do some of these things later. I'm going to look at what they have in the gift shop."

Erik's father excused himself to go to the restroom, and finally Nils and Erik were alone.

"Why didn't you want your picture taken?" Erik asked.

"Because I won't show up in it. You'll be the only one in the picture."

"Why?"

Nils shrugged. "That's just the way it is. Nisser can't be

captured on film. When the pictures come back, you'll just have to cover for me."

That afternoon they went to the Living Seas. Both Nils and Erik liked it so well that they stayed for hours, and Erik's father made a reservation at the Coral Reef Restaurant so they could go on watching the world under the water while they ate.

When a diver who looked like Mickey Mouse started to play with the dolphins, Nils laughed and asked, "What kind of a creature is that?"

"A Disney creature," Erik said. "He's a mouse."

"A mouse with a round button for a nose?"

"Yeah, he's a different kind of mouse."

"I see. He's a different kind of mouse just as I'm a different kind of nisse."

Erik looked at the nisse figure his mother had bought in the gift shop and nodded.

For the next few days, they looked at exhibits, went on rides, and saw shows. They started early in the morning, left to go swimming in the afternoon, and came back early in the evening when the crowds thinned out a bit.

They visited the Disney/MGM Studios and stayed for one night at the Contemporary Resort Hotel, riding into it on the monorail.

Erik learned how to take care of himself in crowds, and he discovered that if he stood up for himself, people wouldn't give him a hard time.

"I'm proud of you, Erik," Nils said. He was invisible now, because they were in the resort hotel getting ready for bed.

"It's not so hard when you know your friend will help you."

"But you did it yourself. I haven't *had* to help you."

"Yeah!" Erik said happily. "I hadn't thought of that, but I guess you're right."

"Erik?" his mother called, "Did you say something?"

"Just talking to myself."

"Back to the earphones," said Nils.

Nils Makes Music

Erik and Nils had just come in from ice skating. Erik's cheeks were bright pink, and he supposed Nils's were, too, but he couldn't be sure. Nils had to stay invisible at the ice rink.

"My earphones are almost frozen to my head!" Erik thought. "The next time we go skating, I'm going off the air."

Nils laughed and said, "If you won't talk to me, I'll hang around with Jenny. She's smart and lots of fun. And didn't she look great in her new red jacket and the hat with the fur trim?"

"Yeah," thought Erik, "but Bobby was skating with her all the time."

"Did you ask her to skate with you?"

"Well, no," Erik admitted.

"What am I going to do with you?" Nils asked. "Your self-confidence was terrific in Florida, but it certainly has fallen apart since we got home."

Erik's mother came into the family room with a cup of hot chocolate. Two marshmallows bobbed up and down in it as she handed it to Erik, and he dipped one out with a spoon. He'd offer it to Nils as soon as she left the room.

"Don't put that down on the table!" she said.

Now he was stuck with holding it—or eating it and saving the other one for Nils. That's what he decided to do.

Nils said, "The one in the cup is mine, right?"

"Right," Erik thought. "But we need another cup for you."

"Will you please remove those earphones for a minute?" Erik's mother said.

Erik did.

"How was the ice?" she asked.

"Just about perfect," Erik said, suddenly wondering what

Nils had used for skates. Maybe he just slid around on the soles of his boots.

"Erik, do you remember our talk about music lessons last summer?"

"Yeah," he said without enthusiasm.

"I know that you didn't want to start in the fall, and I let you postpone it, but if you're going to do it at all, now is the time."

"I don't want to play the violin," Erik said. "Wimps play violins."

He felt a tug at the leg of his jeans and sent a thought message to Nils, "I can't put the earphones on now. She just told me to take them off. Later."

Erik's mother sighed in exasperation. "Well, what *do* you want to play?"

"The trumpet, maybe?" Erik said.

She got up from her chair, annoyed. "I'll discuss it with your father."

As soon as she left the room, Erik put the earphones on and heard, "How about pouring my chocolate? It's not hot anymore, but that's OK."

Erik was surprised to see a small measuring cup appear on the table beside him. He poured into it from the side of his cup and spilled a little. Then he spilled more when the marshmallow splashed. A tissue floated through the air, mopped up the mess, and sailed into the wastebasket.

"Everyone who plays the violin isn't a wimp, you know," Nils said. "Take Ole Bull, for instance."

"Who's he?"

"A violinist—one of the all-time greats. He conducted an orchestra in Oslo and performed with Chopin once."

"Whoever Chopin is," Erik thought.

Nils said, "Your musical education *does* need work. Chopin was a famous Polish composer, but I don't think he wrote anything especially for trumpet."

"I don't care about Ole Bull or Chopin or anybody else! You're *not* going to convince me to play the violin!"

"OK, OK," Nils said. "I just couldn't let that crack about violinists go by. I really liked Ole, and he was *not* a wimp. He came to America in 1852 with eight hundred Norwegians who were going to live on some Pennsylvania land he bought for a dollar an acre, but somebody cheated him. The settlers had to move on west. He played lots of concerts in this country, and everybody loved him."

"How did you get to know him?" Erik thought.

"Oh, some of the nisser around Oslo were playing tricks on him—breaking his violin strings and hiding his rosin. I happened to go to one of his concerts. He came onstage and bowed, and when he started to play, a string broke on the first note. He excused himself, and I was waiting backstage with a new string. After all, I came to hear the music."

"Did he see you?" Erik thought.

"Of course. I wanted him to know that some nisser were civilized, so I introduced myself. I told him that I would take care of his problem."

"And what did he say?"

"He said he'd like to do something for me in return, and I told him I'd let him know when something came to mind."

"How long did it take you to think of something?"

"Years. I decided to visit Bergen, and as I was strolling through a nice, quiet neighborhood, I heard piano music. It was played so well that I expected the musician to be a grownup with a lot of experience."

"And you were wrong, weren't you?" Erik thought gleefully. "I'm starting to figure out how your stories go."

"You're right, I was wrong. It was just a boy. He wasn't much older than you, but he played music fit for the gods of Asgard. His name was Edvard Grieg."

"Oh, yeah, you've been meaning to tell me about him."

"I could tell it better if I had some more hot chocolate," Nils said, and Erik ran to the kitchen to get him some.

"The marshmallows are all gone," thought Erik.

"That's a pity," said Nils. "Next to pop and French fries, they're my favorite thing."

"So what about this Grieg guy?"

"Obviously, he had a great talent. His mother was his teacher, and she was a fine pianist, but she had taught him all she knew. I caught up with Ole Bull and told him I wanted him to come to Bergen and hear young Edvard play."

"Did he?"

"Of course!" Nils said. "He hadn't had a broken string since our meeting, and his rosin was always in his case. He wanted to keep things that way."

"So what did he think about the kid who played the piano?"

Nils said, "He told me that my musical taste and judgment were excellent. He also said he had convinced young Edvard's parents to send him to the Leipzig Conservatory."

"Did Grieg become a famous piano player?"

"No, he was famous for composing music that sounds like Norway. I even helped him with that."

"How?"

"Well," said Nils, "I could see the notes in his mind before he put them on the score. If they weren't going to work out, I erased them."

"Wow!" thought Erik. "Did he know you were around?"

"Sure! I figured he ought to know his collaborator. I made myself visible to him one day when he was sitting on a rock above a fjord looking for inspiration. I pointed out the tiny waterfalls singing down the mountain and said, 'Harp, don't you think?' He agreed. We got to be good friends, and he left a special drawer open for me at Trollhaugen, his home in Bergen."

"What does his music sound like?" Erik thought.

"It sounds the way Norway looks—except for that Arabian dance in Peer Gynt. When we were at Little Norway, I saw a brochure about a musical they do near there in the summer. It's called *Song of Norway,* and the music is by Edvard Grieg."

"Maybe I'll go sometime," Erik thought. "I like music that goes fast. Does he do any of that?"

Nils sang, "Pum pum pum pum pum pum pum!"

"What's that?"

"*In the Hall of the Mountain King.* I can really get into that one!"

"If you liked this Grieg guy so well, why didn't you just stay with him?"

Nils sighed. "I got lonesome for my home near Kristian-sund, but when I went back, the people there simply didn't understand me. Not long after that, I climbed into the chest and sailed for America."

"Lucky for me!" Erik thought.

When Erik's father came home from the bank that night, they had a family conference about his music lessons. His parents agreed to let him try a trumpet if he had his heart set on it.

The next morning, Nils and Erik showed up in the school band room, and Erik told Mr. Taggart, the music teacher, that he'd like to try a trumpet.

Mr. Taggart took Erik's chin in his hand and turned it this way and that, saying, "Hmm. I guess that might be all right for you."

He went to the little cubbyholes that held the instruments and pulled out a black case. A silver horn nestled in the red plush inside.

"Buzz your lips," Mr. Taggart said, showing Erik how to do it.

Erik buzzed, remembering the times when he'd done that with toy cars, running them up and down the sofa.

Finally, Mr. Taggart handed him the mouthpiece of the trumpet and told him to buzz into it. The first time he tried, it tasted nasty, like bitter metal, and he couldn't make a sound.

"Try again," Mr. Taggart said.

The nasty taste was gone this time, and a tiny peep came from the mouthpiece when he buzzed.

"Well," said Mr. Taggart, "you'll just have to keep at it until you get some air into it. Let's put the horn together."

Now Erik made a blatting sound, and Mr. Taggart seemed pleased. When he blew again, he felt pressure on his fingers. The valves went down, and three notes sounded.

Mr. Taggart was surprised, but Erik knew that Nils was at work.

"I'll check this horn out to you," Mr. Taggart said, "and we'll have our first real lesson Thursday."

Erik carried the case proudly, showing it to Jenny. She was impressed.

"Can you play anything on it?" she asked.

"Not yet, but I will," he said. He felt a tug at the seam of his jeans and set the case down to put his earphones on.

Nils said, "I wiped the mouthpiece for you. Did you notice?"

"Yeah," Erik thought. "The rotten taste was gone the second time I blew on it."

"You'll have to practice breathing down deep," Nils said. "Remember Prillar-Guri? The whole valley could hear her, and you should be able to blow at least that well."

Erik buzzed his lips, and when Jenny gave him a funny look, he said, "I'm practicing, OK?"

"Sure, Erik," she said, putting her hand next to his on the case handle. When he turned red, she said, "I was just trying to see how heavy it is."

After school that day, Erik buzzed into the mouthpiece while Nils polished the horn until it shone.

"You'll have to practice every day," Nils said, "even when you don't want to. I remember days when Edvard Grieg really hated to practice, but he did it."

"Why did he do it—if he hated it so much?"

"Because his mother nagged him, and so did I. Your mother will do the same, and so will I."

"Yeah, but I'm not going to be famous or anything—"

"Who knows?" said Nils. "In case you are, you'd better be ready."

Then Nils took the mouthpiece from Erik, fitted it into the horn and played *In The Hall of the Mountain King* so loudly that the chandelier swayed.

"Get visible," Erik begged. "I want to see you play."

Nils materialized and rose on the toes of his boots, playing so enthusiastically that his nisse coat rode up and revealed what was left of his Florida tan.

Nils Hits the Ski Trail

It was Valentine's Day, and Erik was happy because Jenny told him she liked his Valentine the very best of all. She got a lot of them, too. Everybody did. Most kids put one in the box for everyone in the class, but Erik spent a lot of time at the card shop choosing just the right card for Jenny. Nils helped him find one that was pretty and not too mushy.

That night, Erik's father said, "I have some business in Hayward, Wisconsin, about a week from now, and that's the first day of the Birkebeiner. If you can get away, Sonja, I thought we'd all go up and get in on the fun."

"We'd have to take Erik out of school," she said doubtfully.

"Yeah!" said Erik. He felt a tug at the leg of his jeans and put on the earphones.

"What's all this about birch leggings?" Nils asked.

"I don't know what it is," Erik thought, "and I don't care as long as I get out of school."

His father was saying, "You haven't used those cross country skis you got for Christmas very much, but we can take them along. They have a race for kids called the Barnebirkie on Thursday."

"They sure have funny names for things!" Erik said.

His father laughed and said, "They're Norwegian. The Birkebeiner is a race from Hayward to Telemark, and it's like one in Norway. They have it every year to remember the rescue of the prince."

"What prince?"

"I'm a little hazy on that," Erik's father said. "We'll find out when we get there."

"I just hope I don't have a real estate closing then," Erik's mother said.

"If you weren't such a good salesperson, you wouldn't have to worry about that," his father said, giving her a hug. "Ease up!"

69

As Erik was getting ready for bed, Nils said, "Do Americans really ski all the way to Telemark? What do they do about the ocean?"

Erik giggled and thought, "Water ski!"

"Really?" Nils said.

"No, not really. Telemark is the name of a lodge up there. My dad said the race is 55 kilometers. Nils, I'm not very good at skiing. I'd sure hate to enter that race for kids and embarrass my dad."

"You may be better than you think," Nils said, "but I'll take care of it. Ah, the Birkebeiner! It takes me back."

"My dad said it was something about rescuing a prince," Erik thought, "but we'll have to get the story on that later."

"Why later?" Nils asked. "I was there."

"You were?"

"Sure. It was 1206, but I remember it as if it were yesterday. Haakon Haakonsson was just a baby, but certain nasty types didn't want him to grow up to be king."

"So what happened?"

"Two Norwegian soldiers on skis took turns carrying him in a backpack and got him away to a safe place. He grew up to be one of Norway's most famous kings."

"What were you doing there, Nils?"

"Just skiing along beside them talking to the little boy— trying to keep him from being scared. After all, these were two big, hairy guys he didn't even know. They were called birkebeiner because they wrapped birch bark around their legs to keep them warm and dry, and that's where the race gets its name."

"Oh," thought Erik. "It must be hard to ski with a kid on your back."

"Not if you're big and strong," Nils said. "They have a Birkebeiner race in Norway, too, and they make everybody ski with a thirty-five-pound backpack. That's about what little Haakon weighed back then."

For the next week, Erik took his skis to the golf course and practiced. At first, Nils helped him keep his balance and steadied the skis, but then he got the hang of it and did pretty well on his own.

They arrived in Cable in time for the opening ceremonies with marching bands, hot-air balloons, and people from other countries carrying flags.

"It looks like the Olympics!" Erik's mother said.

"I'm going over to check on the Barnebirkie course and see what you have to do to enter," his father said.

He soon came back with a bag full of rosettes all crispy and delicious, dusted with powdered sugar. Erik and his mother each took one, and when they all turned to watch an approaching band, Nils helped himself. Powdered sugar sifted through the air as the rosette disappeared in a few nisse bites.

They drove to Hayward, and when it was close to race time for the Barnebirkie, Erik's father unlashed the skis from the top of the car and handed Erik a race bib that said "Sons of Norway" and "Bill Koch League."

Erik was happy about his number, 99.

They started on the golf course. Erik took his place among kids who looked about the size of his classmates, and one of them said, "You don't belong here. Get back with the little kids."

Erik stuck his chin out and asked, "How old are you?"

"Eleven. What's it to you?"

"So am I," Erik said, poling away from him.

Erik's mother called to him, "Give me those earphones!"

He pretended not to hear, knowing she wouldn't wade through all those kids to take them from him. More than five hundred kids on skis were waiting for the starting signal, many of them sniffing and wiping their noses on the backs of their mittens.

Erik had chosen the 2.5 kilometer race, but Nils said, "Why not do the five kilometers?"

"I don't think I can make it," he thought.

"Well, it's too late now," said Nils. "We're off!"

The day was fairly warm, and the red Klister wax left

71

bloody stains on the snow. Expecting colder weather, Erik had used Polar wax on his skis, and they seemed to drag. The kids he started with passed him by.

"I *told* you to get back where you belong," taunted the boy who had challenged Erik.

Suddenly the kid lost his balance and fell.

Erik grinned and thought, "Nils, did you do that?"

"Somebody had to cut him down to size," Nils said with a merry nisse laugh.

Erik's skis began to move more easily, and he made his way forward with longer glides. Some of the kids were starting to breathe hard as they crossed the golf course. By the time they reached the rear of the elementary school, they were panting. Erik wondered why he wasn't out of breath, but he suspected that he knew the reason.

"Why didn't you ask *me* which wax to use?" Nils asked.

"I didn't know that you knew about such things," Erik thought.

"Ha!" said Nils.

They were coming onto the main street of Hayward and the finish. Erik was pleased with his race and with the medal from the Sons of Norway. He finished somewhere in the middle of the pack, and everybody got a medal. He also got to keep his race bib and planned to hang it in his room.

They went back to the motel to warm up in the whirlpool, and Erik's father said, "I wish I were in shape for the Birkebeiner Saturday."

"How far is that in miles, Dad?"

"About thirty-four miles. The best skiers can make it in two hours and twenty minutes, but others take as long as eight hours to cover the course."

"It seems kind of dangerous to me," said Erik's mother.

"It's not a bit dangerous, Sonja," his father told her. "The National Ski Patrol is out in force, and they have food stations with first aid and ski repair every eight to ten kilometers. Besides, nobody is alone out there."

Erik couldn't wear his earphones in the whirlpool, but he thought, "Nils, are you here?"

The answer was a pinch on his big toe, and Erik thought, "I'll talk to you later."

Back in their room, Erik put on his earphones and locked himself in the bathroom.

"Thanks for helping me in the race," he thought.

"You're welcome. With the right wax, you wouldn't have needed my help."

"Don't rub it in," Erik thought.

"Very funny," said Nils.

"I wish I could do the big race—or even see it."

"That can be arranged."

"The cat chariot?"

"I thought we'd take the goats this time. I'll get in touch with Thor."

Erik filled a motel dresser drawer with towels for Nils. His mother closed it once, but he tip-toed out of bed and opened it again.

"Sorry about that," he thought.

"No problem," said Nils. "If I can spend a century in a

closed chest, I can spend a night in a closed drawer."

Sometime during the night, Erik thought he heard thunder. He sat up in bed, decided that it never thundered in February in Wisconsin, and went to sleep again.

In the morning, Nils said, "I hope Thor didn't wake you last night. He simply can't keep it down!"

The big race began on the main street at nine with seven waves of skiers leaving at five-minute intervals. As they waited for the start, Erik's father said, "You're supposed to start with skiers of your own ability, but everybody thinks they're better than they are."

"Isn't that the truth!" his mother said.

As the first skiers pushed off, the crowds lining the street cheered and yelled. The skiers headed toward the lake, which they would cross and move into the woods. A second group sped after them. The air was filled with excited shouts that made steamy clouds above the heads of the spectators. The sun shone brightly, but it was much colder than the day before—a day for Polar wax.

Erik watched the third wave ski off, then the fourth, fifth and sixth. His earphones were in place under his stocking cap, but Nils had not spoken to him since they left the motel. He was beginning to worry about the nisse.

It was 9:35, and the seventh wave was just pushing off when Nils said, "Walk to the corner and turn left. Your chariot awaits!"

"Should I say something to my folks?" Erik thought.

"No, I'll just stop time."

Erik walked away, amazed that his parents didn't notice, and when he reached the corner, he saw something else that people didn't seem to notice. How could they help but see a chariot of leather and metal with a hitch of eight big, bearded goats? Nils held the reins, which were links of iron.

"Get in," he said.

Erik obeyed, and the goats turned to look at him with huge, golden eyes. They didn't smell bad, but the chariot did

*Nils and Erik fly through the air
in a chariot pulled by eight goats.*

seem to have the odor of hot metal.

"Fasten your seatbelt," Nils said.

"I didn't know these things *had* seatbelts," Erik thought.

"They didn't until you told me about such things."

They were airborne immediately, hovering above the skiers on the frozen lake. Except for their bright racing suits, the skiers looked like a herd of deer on the move.

"Will we be able to see them when they get into the woods?" Erik thought.

"If you don't mind a bit of zig-zagging," Nils said, speaking to the goats in Norwegian.

The chariot moved among the treetops without touching one limb, and Erik looked down on the first station serving donuts and oranges. Not many skiers were stopping this soon, and the ski repair people had nothing to do but watch and cheer.

Erik watched a skier with a French flag on the back of his racing ski suit overtake all the rest, moving ahead with powerful, gliding strides.

"Is he going to win?" he thought.

"It's too early to say," Nils said. "There's a good Norwegian skier back there who might catch him."

"What about the American in the blue?" Erik thought. "He's just as good, and it's *our* race."

"Let's not get nationalistic about this," Nils said. "Why don't we just fast-forward ourselves to Telemark Lodge and find out?"

"OK, but wait a second. I want to see how that lady down there is doing. Do you see her? She looks like Jenny."

Nils looked down and said, "Ah, yes, the one in the pink. She's moving right along. Well, shall we?"

Erik nodded.

Nils spoke to the goats, and they set down in a cloud of powdery snow outside Telemark Lodge. Nils made them invisible, did the same for himself, and they went inside.

"It's 11:15," Nils said. "The best skiers should be coming in."

And so they were. The Norwegian was first, the American was second, and the Frenchman was third. They weren't even breathing hard. They warmed themselves at the lodge fire and congratulated each other.

Others came, including the woman in the pink racing suit who looked like Jenny. When she entered the lodge, somebody yelled, "Three cheers for the winner of the Skade trophy!"

Erik and Nils joined in the "Hip, hip, hooray!"

"Let's fast-forward again," Nils said. "This will go on all day."

Erik saw that it was almost dark, and the last skier was just coming in. A party was in full swing at the lodge, but everyone turned around and cheered when the man dragged himself inside and went to the fire to warm himself. Somebody handed him a steaming cup of coffee, and he said, "It isn't how long it takes, it's whether you get there!"

Nils told Erik, "Now there's something you should remember because it's true."

Then the awards were given. The Norwegian winner received the Haakon Haakonsson award, a bronze casting of a Viking, and the woman in pink got a beautiful stained glass trophy.

As the party resumed, Nils and Erik decided to leave. They found their chariot behind the lodge, where the goats were munching tins that had held baked beans. They looked frightened as Nils approached.

"Why are they scared of you?" Erik thought. "They weren't before."

"Oh, it's that time of day," Nils said. "When Thor gets hungry and can't find food, he kills them and eats them. They know he'll bring them back to life again, but they really hate it when that happens."

"I don't blame them," thought Erik. "Please tell them that I never eat goat."

Nils spoke to the goats in Norwegian. They took their last bites of tin and sprang into the sky.

Erik was startled to find himself standing between his parents at 9:35 in the morning.

"Shall we drive to Cable to see them come in at Telemark Lodge?" his mother asked.

"You and Erik can go," his father said. "I have business to take care of."

"Well, Erik, shall we go?" his mother asked.

"Sure, Mom," he said, "but we can't make it in time to see the winner come in."

"I'll bet we can!" she said.

"How much will you bet?"

"A dollar."

"You're on!" said Erik. He felt guilty about betting against his mother on a sure thing, but he could use the money to buy Nils a treat.

Nils's Farewell

The basketball team won its last game 20-18 with a shot by number nine, Erik Dahl, and everyone was pretty excited about it. Jenny congratulated him and gave him a gumball.

On the way home, Erik thought, "She wouldn't think I was so great if she knew the truth."

Nils said, "Yes, she would."

"But *you* made that shot, Nils."

"Wrong!"

"You mean *I* did it? All by myself?"

"You sure did! I haven't been on that gym floor for weeks."

Erik stopped short. His mouth fell open in amazement. "But I *couldn't* have done it," he thought.

"Of course you could! All you needed was some confidence."

"Come on," Erik thought, "we're going back to the school."

"What for?" Nils asked, "I'm thirsty for lemonade!"

"You'll *get* your lemonade. I just have to try it—now that I know."

Nils shrugged invisibly, and they went back.

The janitor was polishing the gym floor when they got there, and Coach Rolf was putting away some gear.

"Can't get enough of it, can you, Dahl?" the coach said. "You're going to be a standout next season."

"I hope so," said Erik. To Nils, he thought, "Now you stay out of this. I have to find out what *I* can do."

He took a deep breath, let it out, gauged the distance, and went up on his toes to shoot.

"Nice one, Dahl!" said Mr. Rolf as he retrieved the ball.

Erik broke into a wide grin and ran out of the gym.

"See?" said Nils. "You did it!"

Erik thought, "Are you sure that you didn't mess with that ball?"

"Are you kidding? I was sitting on the hoop at the opposite end of the gym! *Now* can we have our lemonade?"

When they got home, Erik's mother was there.

Nils said, "Just put my glass in the bedroom."

Erik hurried to the refrigerator and poured two glasses, setting one on his dresser before he went to the living room to greet his mother. He took his earphones off and put them on the coffee table.

"Hi, Mom!" he said, "We won the game by two points—mine!"

She gave him a hug and said, "You're getting to be quite the athlete. First the Barnebirkie and now this."

"Why are you home so early?" Erik asked.

"I just stopped by to pick up an address I needed. By the way, I finally got that film from Florida developed."

"Let me see!"

As Erik looked at the pictures from Walt Disney World, his mother said, "I could have sworn that I took a picture of you with that nice, little dwarf you met, but it doesn't seem to be there."

"He wasn't a dwarf, Mom."

"Well, whatever he was, he seems to have disappeared."

Erik looked at the picture of himself with his arm around Nils. He looked funny standing in front of a castle with his arm curved around nothing.

When his mother went back to the office, Erik found Nils drinking lemonade in bed. The glass was tilting above the sweatshirts in the drawer.

"You're right," he told Nils. "You don't show up in pictures. But you can show up now. She's gone."

"You know, Erik, I can't stay here with you forever," Nils said.

"Why not? Don't you like living with us?"

"I love it, but somebody else needs me more than you do now. You're in pretty good shape, Erik."

"Yeah, but you're my best friend!"

Hjemkomst (homecoming)
Replica of 1,000-year-old Gokstad Viking ship
Heritage-Hjemkomst Center, Moorhead, Minnesota

"We can still be friends. I'll just go back to Vesterheim and wait for my next assignment, and you can visit me there."

"Don't go until after our vacation," Erik begged.

Nils promised that he wouldn't.

The school year dwindled to weeks and then days. Finally, the Dahls bought a new van and loaded it with suitcases. They were off to visit relatives in Minnesota and the Dakotas.

Erik's mother's relatives, the Loftsgards, lived in Moorhead, Minnesota. After a huge, delicious meal in their house, Erik and his parents were taken to the Heritage-Hjemkomst Center. Lillie Loftsgard, Erik's great aunt, called it "the pride of the Red River Valley."

Right in the middle of everything was a tall Viking dragon ship.

"What a beauty!" Nils said. "I'm trying to think which of my old friends built it."

"None of them," thought Erik. "It says right here that an American junior high school counselor made it. His name was Robert Asp."

Nils was exasperated. "I can see that I'll have to learn to read English if I'm going to stay here."

Great Aunt Lillie was explaining that Mr. Asp got sick and died before he could sail the ship to Norway the way he planned.

"His family and friends got a crew together to sail it home for him," she said. "That's what the name means, 'homecoming'. They sailed that ship from Duluth to Bergen, more than six thousand miles."

Erik's father said, "The center's motto is appropriate—'Dare to Dream.'"

They started into the first interpretive exhibit that told about the land, but Erik turned to look at the dragon ship again.

"Good workmanship," said Nils.

"That tent-top roof looks good over it, too," Erik thought.

Nils said nothing for awhile, and just when Erik was beginning to wonder where he had gone, he saw him. The nisse had shinnied up the dragon's neck. He grinned at Erik and waved, saying, "I should have noticed how new the wood is. White oak, if I'm not mistaken."

"You're right," Erik said. "That's what it says here."

The voices of more visitors warned Nils to become invisible, and Erik went over to watch the videotape on the voyage of the Hjemkomst.

Nils said he didn't want to join him. Just *watching* a ship on the water was enough to make him seasick.

Erik laughed and thought, "Yeah, you wouldn't even ride the Viking ship at Walt Disney World, and that was neat. We ended up in a fjord."

Back at Great Aunt Lillie's house, the women all went to the kitchen to make lefse and other good things for another big meal. Nils and Erik were in the living room trying to think of something to do.

Nils pulled a big, bright magazine out of the rack beside Great Uncle Holger's easy chair and said, "Here's the souvenir program for the Norsk Høstfest. We could check that out while we're waiting for dinner."

Erik looked at the book and thought, "Minot, North Dakota, is pretty far, I think, but that's no problem for you. But it's over—or it hasn't happened yet. It's in October."

"That's no problem, either," Nils said. "Do you want the cats or the goats?"

"The goats, I guess," Erik thought.

"Come on, then," Nils said. "We'll be back in time to eat."

The goat chariot was waiting in the alley behind Great Aunt Lillie's house, and Nils and Erik were airborne immediately. Erik blinked, and when he opened his eyes, the chariot was landing in the Valhalla Hospitality Area.

Happy people were rushing everywhere, buying things, eating Scandinavian goodies and hurrying to performances on the many stages of the All Seasons Arena.

Nils and Erik could have heard Crystal Gayle, the Statler Brothers or Andy Williams, but they decided to catch the act of Bjøro Haaland, the top musical artist of Norway.

Erik laughed and laughed at the idea of country music sung in Norwegian, but Nils got all misty-eyed as he listened to the deep-voiced singer in a cowboy hat.

They looked at a display of Viking weapons, watched a rosemaling demonstration and admired some wood carvings by Harley Refsal from Erik's hometown, Decorah, Iowa. Then the wonderful food in the Oslo Hall Sidewalk Cafe made them so hungry that they decided it must be time to eat at Great Aunt Lillie's house. A lady couldn't finish her cream and bread, so Nils told Erik to grab it. It would be a treat for the goats.

They got back about the same time they left, and Erik finished paging through the souvenir program. He thought, "We were in the past, weren't we, Nils?"

"That's right. Barbara Mandrell might not come next year. I caught her act while you were messing around in the Viking Market."

"Wash your hands and come to the table, Erik," his mother called.

The Dahls continued their trip into South Dakota and did it all— the Badlands, Mount Rushmore, the caves, the mines, Crazy Horse, the dinosaurs, and the Reptile Gardens.

Seeing the dinosaurs, Nils said, "Loki must have had more ugly children than I realized!"

Before they left Rapid City, Erik's mother said she wanted to visit the Chapel in the Hills. They took the Rimrock Road out of town.

Seeing the stave church backed by hills and surrounded by pines, Nils said, "How did that get here? It belongs in Borgund, Norway. As I recall, it was built around 1150."

They went inside, and Erik read about the church, passing the information on to Nils.

"It's a copy, Nils," he thought. "They built it in 1969, but some of the carvings were done in Norway. A man named

84

The Chapel in the Hills
Rapid City, South Dakota

Arndt Dahl gave the money for it to remember his mom and dad."

Erik's mother said, "I wonder if these Dahls are related to us?"

"Could be," said his father.

"Follow me, Erik," said Nils, "I want to show you something."

The nisse pushed a small sliding door to reveal a hole to the outside.

"What's that for?" Erik thought.

"To give Holy Communion to lepers. They weren't allowed in the church. And that roofed walkway outside is where men left their weapons when they came inside. We call it a *svalgang.*"

"This is a pretty small church," Erik thought.

"It's no bigger than it needs to be. Only the old and the sick and the mothers with little children sat down on the benches around the edge. Everybody else stood or knelt."

"You know absolutely everything, don't you, Nils?" Erik thought. "I wish I could quit school and have you be my teacher."

"I'd like that, too," Nils said, "but that's not what the norns are weaving. I'm pleased with your progress and ready to move on."

Erik felt like crying, but he didn't do it.

When they got home, unpacked and put everything away, Erik and Nils had a farewell snack in the bedroom.

"I'll miss those sweatshirts," Nils said with a sigh. "Handwoven things are a lot stiffer."

"I'll give you one to take along," Erik thought.

Nils, who considered it safe to stay visible behind closed doors, shook his head. "No, I'm afraid I have to stay ethnic. Well, do you want to walk me over to Vesterheim?"

"Sure," said Erik aloud. His voice was as sad as could be.

"Don't feel bad," Nils said. "It isn't as if we were saying good-bye forever."

"I know," Erik said, "but I'll miss you."

Nils slapped him on the back and said, "Come on, cheer up! You can bring some rosettes over anytime, and we'll eat them in the storeroom."

"But what if you're off on another assignment?"

"Just leave a thought message, and I'll get back to you."

They left the house and walked toward the museum as slowly as they could. Erik was carrying a small book in his hand.

"If you're going to be as sad as all that, maybe I'd better erase your memory of me," Nils said.

"No!" Erik said, "Please don't do that!"

"Then cheer up," Nils said.

"I will, I will!"

When they were almost to Vesterheim, Erik stopped and opened the book in his hand. He opened it and read, "*Det var hyggelig a treffe Dem.* Is that right? Did you understand?"

"Of course I understood!" Nils said. "It was wonderful meeting you, too."

They stepped behind a big, old tree, and Nils became visible just long enough to shake Erik's hand. Then he entered the museum and went looking for the chest, where he would be rediscovered soon.

Erik blinked rapidly to get rid of any lurking tears. He ran home and threw the Norwegian-American phrase book on the hall table.

"Erik?" his mother called. "I picked up some new batteries for your earphones. The ones you have seem to be dead."

"Yeah," he said. "Thanks, Mom."

He went to his room and flopped down on the bed, feeling just terrible until the phone rang. It was Jenny inviting him to a swimming party at the pool in her backyard.

"Mange takk," he told her, puzzling both Jenny and himself. He had meant to say thanks in English.

He grabbed the earphones from his dresser and put them on, hearing nisse laughter. Or did he hear it? Maybe memory was the magic.

"Whatever," he said, feeling much more cheerful.

As Erik rummaged in a dresser drawer for his swimming suit and rushed out the door, the nisse indentation in the sweatshirts disappeared. The drawer slid shut ever so slowly.

At Vesterheim, Nils opened the lid of the chest decorated with rosemaling. Empty! His covers had been catalogued. He quickly got in touch with Odin's wife, Frigga, who spun so beautifully with her golden distaff and spindle. He told her he needed some bedding as soon as possible because he had to rest up for the three-day Nordic Fest in Decorah the last weekend in July.

A coverlet almost as soft as a sweatshirt appeared in the chest. It was embroidered with the shining apples distributed by Idun, the goddess of youth.

"Thank you, Ma'am," said Nils. He climbed into the chest and snuggled into the coverlet, thinking of the Nordic Fest.

"Rosettes," he said dreamily. "There'll be lots of rosettes with powdered sugar!"

What the Words Mean

Aesir—The three gods Odin, Hoenir, and
   Lodur, who represented Spirit, Will, and
   Warmth.
Angerboda—Loki's ogress wife.
Asgard—Fortress of the gods in the center of
   the earth.
Ask—The ash tree that became man.
Barnebirkie—Ski race for children during the
   February cross-country classic at Hayward,
   Wisconsin.
Birkebeiner—Birch leggings; also the name of
   the annual Hayward ski race.
Embla—The alder tree that became woman.
Ethnic—Designation of a group by its mem-
   bers' ancestry, language, customs, music,
   etc. Norwegian-Americans are an example
   of an ethnic group.
Fax—A machine: A letter or message travels
   many miles by phone line and is printed on
   your own Fax machine. Nisse fax is the
   same but the magic nisser do not need the
   phone wires.
Frey—Norse god of growth and harvest.

Frey
Norse god of growth and harvest

Freyja—Norse goddess of love and beauty.

Frigga—Wife of Odin, the sky god.

Fjord—Also spelled Fiord: narrow inlet of the sea, between cliffs, especially in Norway.

Ginungagap—The deep pit between frozen fog and raging flames in the Norse creation story.

Gnomes—Intelligent dwarfs of the inner earth. They knew all about hidden treasures and rich mines.

Goldbristles—Name of the golden pig that Frey rides.

Gungnir—Odin's spear.

Hardanger Fiddle

Hardanger—Cut embroidery.

Hardanger fiddle—Special Norwegian violins.

Hoenir—Odin's brother, who gave humans the will to think.

Idun—Youth goddess and owner of the golden apples.

Jotun—A giant that hates light.

Kringle—Pastry.

Lefse—A Norwegian bread rolled into thin rounds; baked on a grill; spread with butter, sugar, and toppings; rolled up, and cut into serving pieces.

Lepers—People with leprosy, a disease.

Lodur—Odin's brother who gave humans feelings and warm blood.

Loki—Norse fire god noted for his cunning.

Lur—A horn that can be heard far away.

Mange Takk—Many thanks in Norwegian.

Megahertz—Radio term.

Muspelheim—The place of raging flames in the Norse creation story.

Niflheim—The place of frozen fog in the Norse creation story.

Nisse—Elfin creature capable of good deeds or mischief (pronounced niss-a or niss-uh). Likes barns, kitchens; seldom seen.

Nissedahle—Pioneer Norwegian homestead with stave church at Little Norway near Blue Mounds, Wisconsin.

Nisser—Plural of Nisse; more than one Nisse.

Norns—The three fates who spin the destinies of all.

Norsk Høstfest—Annual Scandinavian fall
   festival in Minot, North Dakota.
Odin—The sky god or Allfather of Norse
   mythology.
Ogre—Folklore's man-eating giant.
Ogress—Female ogre; likes the same diet.
Rosemaling—A style of Norwegian folk art
   painting.
Rosettes—Deep-fried cookies made with a
   special iron.

Nils holds a rosette

Selland Forde—A log house at Vesterheim.

Sif—The golden-haired wife of Thor.

Skuld—One of the three norns. Skuld sees the future.

Sprite—A creature like an elf, fairy, pixie, or goblin, with special powers for good.

Stabbur—A Norwegian storage building.

Stave—Norwegian word for a mighty wooden pillar used in building a church.

Trolls—Ugly, mean, people-like creatures who lived underground or at the bottom of a lake, and came out after dark to help the forest scare the daylights out of nighttime travelers.

Urd—Another of the three norns. Urd sees the past.

Valhalla—Odin's great hall for dead heroes.

Verdande—Another of the three norns. Verdande sees the present.

Ymir—The frost giant who was the first living being.